TORCH

(a *Take It Off* novel)

If you can't take the heat… stay away from the flame.

Katie Parks has been on her own since the age of fifteen. All she's ever wanted is a place to call her own—a life that is wholly hers that no one can take away. She thought she finally had it, but with the strike of a single match, everything she worked so hard for is reduced to a pile of smoking ash. And she almost is too.

Now she's being stalked by someone who's decided it's her time to die. The only thing standing in the path of her blazing death is sexy firefighter Holt Arkain.

Katie's body might be safe with Holt… but her heart is another story.

As the danger heats up, sparks fly, and the only thing Katie knows for sure is that her whole life is about to go up in flames.

TORCH

Take It Off Series

CAMBRIA HEBERT

Published by: Cambria Hebert

http://www.cambriahebert.com

Interior design and typesetting by Sharon Kay
Cover design by MAE I DESIGN
Edited by Cassie McCown
Copyright 2013 by Cambria Hebert

Paperback ISBN: 978-1-938857-25-6
eBook ISBN: 978-1-938857-23-2

DEDICATION

This novel is dedicated to all the firefighters, police officers, US military service members, and all crisis first responders. You are true real-life superheroes that walk amongst civilians. If it weren't for you, the world would be a much darker place.

And, of course, thank you for providing authors like me such delicious inspiration.

TORCH

1

The pungent smell of gasoline stung my nostrils and my head snapped back in repulsion. I opened my eyes and lifted my hands to place them over my mouth and nose to hopefully barricade some of the overwhelming scent.

Except my hands didn't obey.

I tried again.

Panic ripped through my middle when I realized my arms weren't going to obey any kind of command because they were secured behind me.

What the hell?

I looked down over my shoulder, trying to see the thick ropes binding my wrists. The lighting in here was dim.

Wait. Where was I?

My heart started to pound, my breathing coming in shallow, short spurts as I squinted through tearing eyes at the familiar shapes around me. A little bit of calmness washed over me when I realized I was in my home. Home was a place I always felt safe.

But I wasn't safe. Not right now.

I sat in the center of my living room, tied to my dining room chair. I was supposed to be in bed sleeping. The boxers and T-shirt I wore said so.

I started to struggle, to strain against the binds that held me. I didn't know what was going on, but I knew enough to realize whatever was happening was not good.

Movement caught my attention and I went still, my eyes darting toward where someone stood.

"Hello?" I said. "Please help me!"

It was so dark I couldn't make out who it was. They seemed to loom in the distance, standing just inside the entryway, nothing but a dark shadow.

My eyes blinked rapidly, trying to clear the tears flowing down my cheeks. The gasoline smell was so intense. It was like I was sitting in a puddle of the stuff.

"Help me!" I screamed again, wondering why the hell the person just stood there instead of coming to my aid.

The scrape of a match echoed through the darkness, and the catch of a small flame drew my eye. It started out small, reminding me of the fireflies I used to chase when I was a child. But then it grew in intensity, the flame burning brighter, becoming bolder, and it burned down the stick of the match.

The dark shadow held out the matchstick, away from their body, suspending it over the ground for several long seconds.

And then they dropped it.

It fell to the floor like it weighed a thousand pounds and left a small glowing trail in its wake. I watched the flame as it hit the floor, thinking it would fizzle out and the room would be returned to complete blackness.

But the flame didn't fizzle out.

It ignited.

With a great whoosh, fire burst upward, everything around that little match roaring to life with angry orange flames. I screamed. I didn't bother asking for help again because it was clear whoever was in this house wasn't here to help me.

They were here to kill me.

To prove my realization, the dark figure calmly retreated out the front door. The flames on the floor grew rapidly, spreading like a contagious disease up the walls and completely swallowing the front door. The small antique side table by the door, which I'd lovingly scraped, sanded, and painted, caught like it was the driest piece of wood in the center of a forest fire.

Smoke began to fill the rooms, curling closer, making me recoil. How long until the flames came for me?

I began to scream, to call for help, praying one of my neighbors would hear and come to my rescue. Except I knew no one was going to rush into this house to save me. They would all stand out on the lawn at the edge of the street and murmur and point. They would click their tongues and shake their heads, mesmerized by the way the fire claimed my home. And my life.

I wasn't going to die like this.

I twisted my arms, straining against the corded rope, feeling it cut into my skin, but I kept at it, just needing an inch to slip free.

I tried to stand, to run into the back of the house. If I couldn't get loose from the chair, I would just take it with me. But my ankles were crossed and tied together.

I called for help again, but the sound was lost in the roaring of the flames. I never realized how loud a fire truly was. I never realized how rapidly it could spread. It was no longer dark in here, the flames lighting up my home like the fourth of July, casting an orange glow over everything. The entire front entryway and stairwell were now engulfed. I could see everything was doused in gasoline; the putrid liquid created a thick trail around the room. Whoever had been here completely drenched this house with the flammable liquid and then set me in the center of it.

I managed to make it to my feet, hunched over with the chair strapped around me. It was difficult to stand with my ankles crossed. But I had to try. I had to get out of here. I took one hobbled step when a cough racked my lungs. I choked and hacked, my lungs searching for clean air to breathe but only filling with more and more pollution.

I made it one step before I fell over, my shoulder taking the brunt of my fall, the chair thumping against the thickness of the carpet. I lay there and coughed, squinting through my moist and blurry vision, staring at the flames… the flames that seemed to stalk me.

They traveled closer, following the path of the gas, snaking through the living room, filling it up and rushing around me until I was almost completely circled with fire. The heat, God, the heat was so intense that sweat slicked my skin, and it made it that much harder to breathe.

It was the kind of heat that smacked into you, that made you dizzy and completely erased all thought from your brain.

I was going to die.

Even if I were able to make it to my feet, I wouldn't be able to make it through the circle of fire that consumed everything around me.

I pressed my cheek against the carpet, not reveling in its softness, not thinking about the comfort it usually afforded my bare feet. Another round of coughing racked my body. My lungs hurt. God, they hurt so bad. It was like a giant vise squeezed inside my chest, squeezed until all I could think about was oxygen and how much I needed it.

My chin tipped back as I writhed on the floor, making one last attempt at freedom before the flames claimed me completely. I heard the sharp crackling of wood, the banging of something collapsing under the destruction, and I blinked.

This is it.

The last moments of my life.

I'm going to die alone.

I started to hallucinate, the lack of oxygen playing tricks on my fading mind, as a large figure stepped through the flames. Literally walked right through them. He held up his arms, shielding his face and head as he barreled through looking like some hero from an action movie.

My eyes slid closed as my skin began to hurt, like I sat outside in the sun for hours without the protection of sunscreen.

I heard a muffled shout and tried to open my eyes, but they were too heavy. Besides, I preferred the darkness anyway. I didn't want to watch as my body was burned to death by fire.

Pain screamed through me and the feeling of the carpet against my cheek disappeared. My first thought was to struggle, but my body couldn't obey my mind. I felt movement, I felt the solidness of someone's chest, and I could have sworn I heard the sound of a man's voice.

"*Hang on,*" he said.

The shattering of glass and the splintering of wood didn't wake me from the fog that settled over my brain. The scream of pain at my back, the extreme burning and melting that made a cry rip from my throat still wasn't enough to get my eyes to open.

And then I could hear the piercing wail of sirens, the faraway shouts of men, and the muffled yell of one who was much closer.

I really thought heaven would be more peaceful.

And then I was sailing through the air, the solid wall of whatever held me ripped away. I plunged downward, and with a great slap, I hit water, the icy cold droplets a major shock to my overheated system.

My eyes sprang wide; water invaded them as I tried to make sense of what was happening. I thought I was burning. But now I was... drowning.

The water was dark and it pulled me lower and lower into its depths. I looked up. The surface rippled and glowed orange. I almost died up there. But I would die down here now.

I wanted to swim. My arms, they hurt so badly, but they wanted to push upward, to help me break the surface toward the oxygen my body so desperately needed.

But I was still tied to a chair.

The chair hit the ground—a solid, cold surface— as my hair floated out around me and bubbles discharged from my nose and mouth.

It wasn't hot here.

It wasn't loud, but eerily quiet.

It was a different kind of death, but death all the same.

The ripples in the water grew and the chair began to rock. I heard the plunge of something else coming into the water and I looked up. Through the strands of my wayward hair, I saw him again. My hero. His powerful arms pushed through the water in three great stokes. He reached out and grabbed me beneath the shoulder, towing me upward toward the bright surface.

When my head cleared the water, my lungs automatically sucked in blissful air. It hurt so bad, but it was the kind of pain I had to endure. Another cough racked my body, and as I wheezed, the man towing me and my chair through the water said, "Keep breathing. Just keep breathing."

And then I was being lifted from the water, the chair placed on the cement as I coughed and wheezed and greedily sucked in air.

"Ma'am," someone was saying. "Ma'am, can you hear me? Are you all right?"

I looked up, blinking the water out of my eyes, but my vision was still blurry. I tried to speak, but all I could manage was another cough.

The ropes around my wrists were tugged, and I cried out. The pain was so intense that I thought I would pass out right there.

"Stay with me," a calm voice said from behind. It was the same voice that instructed me to keep breathing.

When my arms were free, I sagged forward. The pain splintering through me was too much to bear. And then there were hands at my ankles; I heard the knife against the rope. When I was completely untied, my body fell forward, sliding off the chair and toward the ground.

But he was there.

I slid right into his arms, my body completely boneless.

A low curse slipped from his lips as he yelled for a medic. Yeah, a medic. That seemed like a good idea. I hurt. I hurt all over.

I cried out when he shifted me in his arms, bringing me closer to his chest. I pressed my face against him. He was wet, but his clothes were scratchy against my cheek. I tried to look at him; I opened my eyes and tilted back my head. I caught a flash of dark hair and light eyes, but then my vision faded out, pain took over, and I passed out.

2

The problem with passing out is that upon awakening, you had to face the pain of whatever caused you to pass out in the first place all over again. Okay, so the pain wasn't as bad as it was before, and I figured that was in large part due to the IV sticking out of the back of my hand. I wish they had a pain pill for that because IVs hurt.

I blinked, trying to focus and look around the room. I was in a private room, which was nice. The walls were sterile white; there was a curtain pushed open around the bed and a TV mounted to the wall. The blankets that covered me to my waist were no nonsense and kind of scratchy. Not at all like my pillows and bedding at home.

Home.

The thought brought up a surge of panic. I looked down at my wrists, which were wrapped in layers of white gauze that wound down around the base of my thumbs and then back up again.

Burned.

I was burned.

Images from what happened assaulted me. The match, the fire, the fear. I shifted, wanting to get away from the memories, and a lock of hair slid onto my cheek. It smelled like smoke.

The memory of almost choking to death on smoke made a sound tear from the back of my throat. The monitor off to my right began to beep, and I looked up, the sound helping a little to bring me back to reality.

I was safe.

There was no fire here.

There was no man standing in the shadows with a match.

The door to my room opened and a nurse bustled in. She smiled when she saw me looking at her. "Ah, you're awake. I'll get the doctor." She pressed a couple buttons on the monitor, and the rapid beeping stopped; then she hurried from the room.

There was a dull ache in my shoulder and my skin felt tight everywhere, like it got wet and I was thrown in the dryer, which caused it to shrink around my body. I glanced down at the bandages around my wrists again and wondered how good the drugs they had me on were. As in, how bad was this going to hurt later when I wasn't taking as much medicine?

I glanced at the water pitcher next to the bed, wondering if there was any water in it. My throat felt so dry, like I hadn't had any water in days… How long had I been lying here?

I stretched out my arm, reaching for the pitcher, but I didn't make it very far because every single muscle in my arm and back groaned in protest. But instead of flopping my arm back down, I sat frozen, staring at the red burn on my right hand. The skin was completely crimson, like I stuck my hand out a window and let it roast an entire day in the hot southern sun.

I got burned in the fire.

My brain seemed to be working extra slow because that was just now becoming clear. The bandages obviously hadn't been enough of an indicator. And the fact that my wrists were bandaged and my hands were not but were still red… Well, that was very telling. Those burns must be worse.

The door to my room opened again. I glanced up expecting a doctor in a white lab coat, carrying a chart. But it wasn't a doctor. It wasn't a kind-faced nurse either.

The door swung slowly shut behind him and his footsteps paused when he saw I was staring at him. As if I could look away. Once again, I felt the familiar feeling of my lungs seizing from lack of oxygen. It was like he was some extreme human vacuum that had the ability to suck every ounce of air out of the room.

"You're awake." His voice was oxygen to my breathless body. The minute the calm yet strong words passed his lips, my body automatically inhaled. It's almost like my body knew him—like it recognized him even though my brain screamed it would never forget a single thing about his incredible face. And his words… Did that mean he hadn't accidentally stumbled into the wrong room on the way to visit his sick and frail grandmother?

Who was I kidding? He didn't look like the type that would have a sick and frail anything.

He was tall, obscenely taller than I was... He probably stood over six feet (that put him an whole foot taller than me) with very wide shoulders that gave way to lean hips and legs that seemed to go on for miles, only to end with feet the size of Florida. How he found boots to contain those things I would never understand.

Along with his scuffed-up tan boots, he was wearing jeans, a worn gray T-shirt (untucked), and an army-green jacket with about a million pockets on the front. He was dressed like any ordinary guy you would see on the sidewalk or at the mall.

Except he was anything but ordinary.

He was ruggedly casual. He had the kind of look that women of any age would follow with their eyes until he was completely out of sight. It was almost as if he put not a single thought into the way he stepped out of the house.

His dark hair was short but still appeared rumpled. His very strong jaw was covered in stubble, creating a shadow over the bottom part of his face. Above the stubble was a strong nose, heavy dark brows, and eyes... light-blue eyes that seemed out of place with such dark hair and olive-toned skin.

Yet, they weren't out of place. They were a beacon. Somewhere to focus. Somewhere for my suddenly tilted world to be grounded.

"Are you thirsty?" he said, noticing I was turned and reaching toward the pitcher. He cleared his throat and came quickly across the room, snatching up the pitcher and frowning. "It's empty."

I watched, still unable to say a word, as he disappeared into the bathroom where I heard the faucet begin to run. I finally dropped my arm back onto the bed, wincing a little at the pain but feeling more awake than I had since opening my eyes.

The faucet shut off and he strode back into the room, my eyes once again fastening on his face, on his fluid, strong movements. I had no idea who he was, but I certainly enjoyed looking at him. Something began to uncoil in my middle—something warm and pleasant. A feeling that eclipsed the pain and fear of waking up in a hospital room alone and unclear.

"Here," he prompted softly, placing a straw in the small yellow cup and holding it close to me. His scent wafted close, completely taking over my senses and making me forget my throat was as dry as a desert. It was deep and clean. Very manly. Very powerful without being overwhelming. He cleared his throat, using his thick fingers to bend the straw toward my mouth as he held it still.

My lips parted and the straw found its way between my lips, but my eyes, my stare was held captive by his icy-blue irises. Icy eyes that were far from cold. My body seemed to remember how dry it felt because without me realizing, I drew some water through the straw. It was almost painful going down, and I felt it travel all the way through my throat and spread into my stomach.

I coughed a little, the lukewarm liquid a little startling to my system, and the cup disappeared and the incredibly handsome stranger moved closer, sliding his arm around my shoulder and staring down at me with concern-laced eyes.

"Does anyone know you're awake?"

"Wh-who are you?" I said. My voice was unusually throaty and low.

The door to my room opened once more. Geez, couldn't a girl get any privacy with some hottie stranger? It was a fun thought... until I remembered that someone tried to kill me. A stranger.

I jerked away from his touch, biting back a cry of pain.

He straightened and moved away as the doctor moved to the end of the bed, first glancing up at the monitor, which was once again beeping wildly, and then back at me with a polite expression on his face. The nurse was right behind him, coming around to silence the machine once more.

"Miss Parks, it's good to see you awake. Are you in any pain?"

"Not too much," I replied, noticing again at the deep tone of my voice. My hand automatically went to my throat.

"The change to your voice is only temporary. You inhaled quite a bit of smoke. You will likely have a sore throat for a while."

"My hands," I said, looking up at him.

"How much do you remember?" the doctor asked.

I felt the stranger's attention sharpen as he stared at me, waiting for my answer. I glanced at him, unsure if I should be talking to my doctor about anything in front of him.

"I'll just wait outside, in the hall," he said, clearly noticing my discomfort.

The doctor nodded, but I had to know. "Should I know you?"

He stopped and pivoted. "No, I..." His words trailed away like he wasn't sure how to explain the fact that he was here.

"He's the fireman who pulled you out of the house," the nurse said, excitement lacing her tone like this was some huge scene in one of the soap operas she likely watched.

The doctor cleared his throat and gave her a look full of reproach, and she glanced at the floor guiltily.

Images of the raging fire flashed before me. I felt the heat, the claws of death reaching for me… but then I saw the man—the one I thought had been nothing but a hallucination. He stepped through the flames. He literally walked through a wall of fire to pick me up and carry me to safety.

He was the one who threw me into the pool. While I was tied to a chair.

"You're him," I said, not asking because the nurse just said so. She was only too thrilled to spill the beans, so I knew it had to be true.

He nodded.

"Stay," I heard myself saying. *Wait, what?*

He didn't move back into the room. Instead, he leaned against the wall, stuffing his hands into the front pocket of his jeans. I mean, seriously, he looked like he could be in a magazine. Advertising some sexy cologne or perfume. Something by the name of *Rogue*.

Oh my God, the fire must have melted half my brain cells. I was daydreaming about perfume after waking up from attempted murder.

"Someone tried to kill me," I told the doctor, looking him straight in the face. The stranger against the wall stiffened but otherwise said nothing, and I didn't look his way.

"So you remember the fire," he said, not directly avoiding my words.

"I remember someone trying to burn me alive."

The doctor frowned and glanced at the nurse, who bustled out of the room quietly. "You can speak with the police about that," he said. "I'm here to focus on your injuries."

"How bad are the burns?"

"You have first and second-degree burns, Miss Parks. I would say you were actually very lucky. You have suffered moderate smoke inhalation. As I said, your throat and voice will be affected for a while. You were on oxygen for the first twenty-four hours that you were here, so breathing shouldn't be a problem."

"Wait," I said, "how long have I been here?"

"Four days."

"Four…" I lost four days. Almost an entire week. That was almost as scary as nearly dying. It was like I did die for four days… four days I would never remember. Four days of being immobile and lost.

"You were very lucky," the doctor said, interrupting my momentary freak-out.

"Lucky?"

"Your injuries are not serious considering the extent of the fire." He glanced at the stranger and then back at me. "You have first-degree burns in places on your hands and second-degree burns on your wrists. We kept you heavily sedated for the first couple days to keep you comfortable. But I'm afraid there is still going to be pain. Your skin is damaged. There may be scarring. We are keeping it clean and medicated with antibiotics to help with infection. The dressings must be changed every eight hours. Unfortunately, this will aggravate the pain. The burns on your hands are considerably less and should heal much faster. I'd like to keep you here for another day and, baring no complications or sign or infection, you can leave. I will prescribe you pain medicine for the pain and the nurse will go over how to change your dressings." He paused with his bad news, then said, "Miss Parks, is there someone that we can contact for you? A relative, a spouse? Someone who will be able to help you during the next few weeks?"

I wanted to say yes. I didn't want to see the flash of pity that would surely creep into his eyes when I said no. But there was no one. There hadn't been for a very long time.

"No."

"I see. Well, in that case, you can come by twice a day to have your bandages changed by the staff."

"I can manage," I said a little too harshly.

He nodded curtly. "I would like to examine you now, if that's okay?"

I nodded.

"I'll wait outside," the stranger said and then disappeared.

I suffered through the exam, barely able to concentrate on the doctor or his invasive questions. I couldn't help but keep glancing at the door, wondering if he had left. Wondering if I would see him again.

After the doctor finished torturing me and poking at the huge bruise covering my shoulder and upper arm (likely from when I fell over in the chair), he took his leave, but not before promising to come back later. Oh, joy.

I heard the deep baritone of a man talking and the doctor giving a short reply. Before the door could completely close, it was pushed open and a dark head appeared. "Can I come in?"

I nodded.

He was carrying a new pitcher of water, identical to the one sitting beside the bed. He gestured toward it. "The nurse gave me some fresh water with ice. It's probably better than the tap water I gave you," he said sheepishly.

I was embarrassed to realize I would have drunk sewer water if he were offering it to me.

I watched as he poured me a new glass and transferred the straw from the old cup into the new one and extended it to me. I took it, though curling my fingers around it proved to be harder than I thought, but I did it, proud that I didn't wince at the pain of my skin stretching over bone.

He regarded me through those crystal-blue eyes as I drank down half of the water. It was icy cold and felt like little needles against my throat, but I continued to drink, my body greedily demanding more.

When I was finished, he took the cup without me asking and placed it on a table that he wheeled right up near my lap.

"You're a fireman?" I asked. "You're the one who...?"

He nodded. "I'm a firefighter."

"You threw me into a pool." I scowled.

He grinned. "You were on fire."

"Well, there is that," I allowed. Talking to him was entirely too easy. Looking at him was entirely too easy. I couldn't forget the reason he was here. "You saved my life."

"All in a day's work," he said, giving a little shrug.

"Should I call the nurse?" I asked.

Alarm wiped the barely there smirk off his face and stiffened his posture. He leaned a little closer, those eyes sweeping over my body. "Are you in pain?"

"We might need something for swelling," I replied. "I've never seen anyone's head grow so much so fast." Was I flirting?

Oh my God, I was totally flirting.

Relief filled his eyes and he grinned. His teeth were bright against the dark of his scruff. "Think she'd give me a sponge bath too?"

The image of him naked and dripping wet with water had the stupid monitor beeping all over again. I hated that stupid thing.

He glanced between me and the monitor, a sly smile curving his lips. When the nurse came in and pressed the button and checked the screen, he winked at me.

He winked.

That small gesture had me clenching my thighs together beneath the scratchy blankets.

After the nurse warned him about too much excitement (I was going to die of embarrassment), we were alone again.

"I have to say…" His eyes gleamed. "You are much more amusing when you're awake."

"This isn't the first time you've been here?" I said, all trace of flirting aside.

"I've been a couple other times."

"A couple?"

He shrugged nonchalantly.

"But why?" I blurted before my manners could rear their ugly head.

He seemed to balk at that question, like he wasn't really sure what to say or how to say it.

"I get it," I told him. "It's like some fireman follow-up policy? Checking in to make sure the victim is okay?"

"Yeah, just following up."

I nodded. "As you can see, I'm going to be fine."

"You told the doctor someone tried to kill you."

"Well, I didn't tie myself to the chair and light my house on fire."

His fists clenched at his sides, like my words made him angry. The muscles in the side of his jaw ticked—a movement I found very distracting.

"Who would try to kill you?" he asked after a few moments.

"That's exactly what we would like to know as well," said a new voice as someone swept into the room.

It was two cops. One female, one male. I had no doubt in my mind that whenever they interrogated someone, the blonde played the good cop and the short, stalky man played the bad cop. "Katie Parks?" the man asked, looking at me.

"Yes."

"We're here to discuss the events from four nights ago."

"That's my cue to leave," the fireman said from my side.

I would much rather talk to him than the police.

"And you are?" the female police officer said, pulling out her pad and pen like she was going to write it down. I knew she wasn't going to. She just wanted to know his name. I really couldn't blame her.

"Holt. Holt Arkain"

His name sizzled me like a bolt of lightning straight to the heart. I'd never heard that name before, but it fit him so well. Strong yet rugged... casual yet unique.

"You're the guy who pulled her from the fire," the male cop said.

Holt nodded.

"You know the victim?"

"Uh, no. I was just..." He glanced at me. "Following up to make sure she was okay."

Something about the way he said it made me think he was here for more than that. But it must have been the pain meds because the officers nodded and then he was walking out the door... I would probably never see him again.

"Holt?" I said, liking the way his name seemed to slip right into my vocabulary.

He stopped his retreat and looked over his shoulder at me. "Yes?"

"Thank you. For saving my life."

There it was, that cocky grin again. "My pleasure."

And then he was gone. I couldn't help but notice how the "good cop" suddenly looked like the bad one. Perhaps she'd been hoping for his phone number.

I felt a little gleeful knowing she wasn't going to get it.

Of course, I likely would never see him again either.

All trace of glee went away. In fact, I wave of weariness washed over me. The officer cleared his throat and looked at me expectantly. I didn't know what I could tell them. I didn't know anything.

The only thing I knew for sure was that someone wanted me dead.

3

As it turned out, I learned a lot more from the police officers than they learned from me. They stayed in my room for almost an hour, asking me question after question. *Do you have any enemies? Did you see the arsonist who set fire to your home? Why didn't you wake up when they dragged you from your bed and tied you to a chair? Who could want to kill you?*

On and on the questions went.

I didn't have an answer for any of them. The honest truth was I had no enemies (that I knew of), I couldn't see the person with the match, and I also really wanted to know why I didn't wake up while being tied to chair. The most logical thing I could come up with was that this was some random act of violence carried out by some seriously unbalanced psycho.

After listening to me repeat my answers over and over, I think the police were coming around to my way of thinking as well. It could have been a burglary gone wrong. It could have been a stupid prank that got out of hand. It could have been a million and one things—all of which made me extremely exhausted to think about.

When the nurse finally ordered them out of my room I was practically in tears. I hated crying. It was a useless waste of energy. Energy that could be better spent doing something that would actually help my situation.

And the situation was pretty grim.

My home was completely destroyed.

According to the police, there was nothing left to salvage.

I did have insurance that would likely cover the home and everything inside, but that really didn't make me feel any better. Everything I owned was gone. The life I built for myself, the life I wanted so badly, was now reduced to a pile of blackened ash.

You'll just start over, I told myself in an effort to lift my spirits. It didn't work. Starting over was something I hated. I had done it so often in the past few years that doing it again made me want to scream bloody murder.

Bloody murder. Okay, that was a bad choice of words.

The idea of starting over again made me want to punch a whole bunch of people in the face.

Yeah, that was better.

If I focused on the anger inside me, I wouldn't have room to think about how utterly devastating it felt to lose everything. I really thought I finally found my place in the world. It hadn't been a large place, but it was mine and that meant more to me than anything.

But with the single strike of a match, everything I ever wanted was consumed by flames.

I drifted off into a fitful sleep, the memory of the fire taunting my subconscious. Just when the memories threatened to choke me, a man with icy-blue eyes appeared and like a bucket of water, his mere presence doused me—extinguishing the worst of my fear.

As the night wore on, pain began to throb. It felt like my skin was on fire all over again—it burned and tingled. I wanted to rip at the bandages and just scrape off the tender, damaged skin until there was nothing left of my wrists but bone. The skin on my hands screamed at me, feeling tight and puckered. All I could do was lie there and wonder how long the pain was going to last. When would I know some relief?

When the sun rose, I decided I wasn't going to even pretend to sleep anymore and I pushed the button for the nurse.

"The pain," I told her when she appeared, "it's worse than yesterday."

She nodded empathetically. "That's because the doctor has lowered the dose of pain medication you're on—you were on a much higher dose when you arrived."

"So the pain isn't going to go away?"

She frowned. "You will be feeling some pain. Burns are very painful. But it's about time for your regular dose, so I can give you that. Once it kicks in, I'm going to have to change your bandages."

I bit back a groan. She was only doing her job; I wasn't going to make her feel bad for it.

True to her word, just as I was getting some relief from the pain, she appeared carrying clean bandages and some supplies. "Look who I found out in the hall," the nurse said, propping open the door with her foot.

It opened wide when Holt shouldered through, his eyes going straight to the bed where I lay. I reached up to brush the hair out of my eyes, taking a moment to worry about the way I looked before stinging pain reminded me I was an idiot for worrying about the way I looked.

He appeared beside me soundlessly and brushed back the tangled hair, tucking it behind my ear. But instead of pulling away, he trailed his fingertips lightly across my cheek over to the bridge of my nose where he trailed them downward before lifting his hand away.

"You have a million freckles," he said, those icy eyes looking anything but frozen.

My stomach did a summersault. "Curse of a redhead," I replied, my voice scraping from my throat. Geez, could I be any more unsexy?

The nurse didn't say anything, but I felt her stare and I tore my eyes away from him to peek at her. She was watching us as she placed all her supplies on the small rolling table beside me.

"Is this a bad time?" Holt asked, not once looking away from my face.

"You're just in time for the torture," I replied.

"I'll be as gentle as I can," the nurse said, settling beside me. "Maybe it's good he's here. He can distract you from the discomfort."

"You're in pain?" he said, his glacial eyes sharpened. His full, kissable lips pulled into a straight line, like the idea of me being in pain made him unhappy.

"It's not so bad," I said, realizing I didn't want him to see how much it hurt.

"I'm just going to remove the bandages, apply this antibiotic, and then rewrap it," the nurse said, drawing away my attention.

Holt grabbed a chair and pulled it up beside the bed, sitting down and propping those humungous feet of his up on the end of the mattress.

"Your feet are huge," I blurted.

He grinned. "You look like you're twelve."

"I do not!"

He face grew serious. "How old are you anyway?"

"Asking a lady her age is impolite," the nurse said as she peeled away what was left of the bandage.

If he replied, I didn't hear. All my attention was sucked down onto my wrist. It looked like a package of raw hamburger. Shiny, raw hamburger. In some places, the skin was bubbled up and loose; in others, the skin was completely gone, leaving behind nothing but red, fleshy-looking parts. The air brushed over it, and I bit down on my lower lip. I never knew air had the ability to inflict pain.

"It's going to look real bad, but that's just the skin's way of healing. Don't be upset by what you see."

But I was upset. It looked awful and it felt worse. I knew it would heal, and I didn't care about the scars it would leave behind, but in that moment, my injuries were a reminder of everything I endured— everything I lost.

I stared down at the mess as the nurse went about cleaning the area and applying the antibiotic. A fine sheen of cold sweat broke out over my forehead and my stomach turned.

Something warm and solid landed on my thigh. I could feel the heat of it even through the blankets that covered my legs. My eyes moved away from the burn and toward the hand that was lying in my lap. Slowly, my gaze traveled up his arm, past his shoulder and unshaven jaw to collide with his eyes. His thumb drew a lazy circle over the blanket, and I forgot about everything else going on around me.

If a single touch from him could make the entire world fall away, then what would his kiss be like?

"So will you smack me if I ask you how old you are again?" he said. I stared at his mouth as he formed the words.

I shook my head. "I'm twenty-two."

His fingers tightened around my thigh for a second before relaxing once more. "That's good."

Why was that good? "How old are you?"

"Twenty-four."

"Almost done," the nurse said. I had completely forgotten she was there. I looked back at my wrist, thankful it was already being covered with a fresh bandage. "One more to go," she said, moving around the other side of the bed.

Holt pushed away and stood up. Instantly, my thigh missed the warmth of his palm. "I'll explain what I'm doing with this one so you'll know what to do when you're released tomorrow."

I nodded as he moved around to the side the nurse just left.

"Who will you be staying with? When they get here, I'll gladly come in and explain to them how to change these. It would be easier for someone with two hands to use."

"I'll be staying by myself," I said, watching as she revealed the other wrist. This one looked exactly the same. "I'll be able to do this, though."

The nurse glanced up, pity flashing into her eyes. I hated it. "You're going to be alone?"

I wonder what she would say if I told her I'd pretty much been alone since the age of fifteen. Instead, I just nodded.

She frowned. "Maybe I should speak to the doctor. Perhaps delaying your release would be best."

"No!" I said quickly. "That isn't necessary. Thank you. I'll be just fine."

"But we don't normally release burn victims without someone to help them."

Burn victim. Her words made my ears ring. I was a burn victim. Someone tried to kill me. I had no idea why.

Before I could tumble into that black hole of worry, Holt's voice pulled me back. "Where are you going to stay?"

I hadn't really thought about it. It was hard to wrap my head around the thought that my little house was gone. I'd only gotten to live there for barely a year. "A hotel, I guess," I replied.

He frowned.

The nurse began explaining what to do with the bandages and medicine. I paid attention, blinking back the tears that threatened to spill onto my cheeks. I was no baby, but this hurt. The kind of pain I hoped I never had to feel again.

The doctor came in as the nurse collected her supplies. He stopped at the foot of my bed and stared down at me the way he had yesterday. "I received some of your lab results." He looked over at Holt before continuing.

"It's okay. He can stay," I said. I knew I barely knew him (okay, I didn't know him at all), but there was something about him that just made me comfortable.

"You had traces of gamma hydroxybutyric acid, commonly known as GHB, in your blood stream."

"Isn't that the date rape drug?" I asked, confused. Then a whole other kind of alarm swamped me. Oh my God, was I raped? Immediately, I started to pay attention to certain parts of me… like the parts between my legs. Did it feel different? Did I feel different? Why hadn't I thought of this before? I had no clue how I ended up tied to that chair in my living room… What else did I not remember?

Holt shot up from his seated position and paced over to the window. Both hands were fisted at his sides.

My mouth opened, but no sound came out. How did you ask a doctor if someone raped you?

The doctor cleared his throat. "As far as I could tell, you were not raped, Miss Parks."

I expelled a breath, relief making me weak. "I don't understand," I murmured.

"The drug is fairly common, easy to get ahold of. It can render the victim unconscious and can also strip away memories—Miss Parks, did you knowingly ingest GHB?"

"No!" I demanded. That was absolutely ridiculous.

The doctor nodded. "I thought as much, but I had to ask. Did you go out to, say, a bar the night before the fire?"

I laughed. "No. I don't go to bars. I didn't go anywhere when I got home from work."

"Where do you work? Is it likely that someone could have slipped it into your drink in your office?"

"I work in a library. I'm a librarian. So no, it's very unlikely."

"I see. Well, I had to inform the police of the toxicology screen. They will likely have questions. The drug is out of your system and there seems to be no ill effects from ingesting it. I can have your release papers ready this evening. Who will you be staying with?"

Why did they all keep asking me this? "I'll be staying by myself."

The doctor seemed to balk at that. "Perhaps a few more days here," he began.

"That isn't necessary. I'll be fine."

"I'm afraid I cannot in good conscience let you leave here alone."

"She won't be alone," came his voice by the window.

Both the doctor and I looked his way as Holt turned, spearing me with those light eyes. "She can stay with me."

"Absolutely not," I protested, my skin flushing at just the thought.

"I think that's a wonderful idea. You need someone to help you," the doctor lectured.

I didn't need help. Not from anyone. I was very good at taking care of myself. I told them both that. What a bunch of Neanderthals.

"I'm afraid if you want to leave this evening, it will have to be on the condition that you not be alone. Otherwise, you can stay here and I will discharge you at the beginning of the week."

Shit. I really didn't want to be here any longer than I had to. Plus, I had to call the insurance company, go back to work, and start looking for another place to live.

"How do you know you aren't releasing me to some crazy person?" I asked the doctor.

He chuckled. "Miss Parks, I have known Mr. Arkain here for several years. He has an impeccable reputation in the community."

I glanced at Mr. Impeccable. "So you take girls home from the hospital often, then?" Something that felt suspiciously like jealousy slithered up my spine.

A slow grin spread over his features. "Nope. You're my first."

The doctor seemed to think this was a done deal and excused himself, promising to return later with my release papers.

Holt strolled over to my bedside, standing over me, staring down.

"I don't like it when people loom over me," I snapped.

"I'm not looming."

"I'm not going home with you."

He smiled.

If my hands weren't burned, I would punch him.

He leaned down close, his breath fanning out over my cheek. "Don't worry, Katie. I don't bite. Unless you want me to."

Before I could react, he was pulling open the door and glancing over his shoulder. "I'll be back tonight to get you."

I had two realizations once he was gone:

One, I hadn't thought about the pain at all when he talked to me.

And, two, I actually kind of wanted to go home with him.

4

The nurses were gossiping about me. Or maybe it was Holt they were in a little frenzy over. Either way, I became the main attraction for several bored nurses. They kept coming into my room, making a fuss over me, and saying how lucky I was that Holt was watching out for me.

It was like I was a stray kitten that someone found on the side of the road that somehow ended up in a wonderful home.

I didn't really want all the attention, but I did use it to my advantage (like you wouldn't), and one of the nurses washed my face and hair, going as far as finding a blow dryer and drying it into a long, straight style. It took her forever because my hair was so thick and long, but she didn't seem to mind. In fact, I think she kind of liked it. She said it got her out of emptying bedpans.

By the time my hair was done, I was tired, the pain meds were wearing off again, and I just wanted to go to sleep to escape reality for a little while. As I lay there in the quiet of my room, my mind kept wandering to Holt.

Part of me didn't think he would come back. The other part of me kept looking at the door, waiting for him. For a girl who learned early in life not to depend on anyone, I sure was acting like I was thinking about depending on him.

I didn't know what possessed him to announce that he was taking me home. He had to know I wasn't going anywhere with him. Still, I was going to let the doctors think I was because it was my fastest way out of here.

I'm just part of his job, I reminded myself. *The only reason he's been coming here is because he's a firefighter—a man who cares about the wellbeing of others.*

I fell asleep for what could have been hours or minutes and was awakened by the soft weight of something settling on the end of the bed.

It was a bag. A shopping bag with the mall's logo on the side. I yawned and sat up a little straighter, eyeing the bag.

"I thought you might want something to wear that didn't smell like smoke and had a little more... coverage."

I remembered the boxers I was wearing when he pulled me out of the house and blushed. I divided my glance between the bag and the man who brought it. He must never shave. Either that or he was secretly a werewolf who grew facial hair at the speed of light. "You brought me clothes?"

"It's just a pair of jeans and a T-shirt. I didn't know what size you wear, so I had to guess."

He brought me clothes. It was a small gesture, but it proved that he thought about me even after he left this room. "Thank you." I smiled. "I really wasn't looking forward to putting on those smelly boxers."

He grinned. "The nurses out in the hallway said you were all ready to go."

I pushed back the covers and swung my legs over the bed. "Yes, the doctor cleared me to leave. I'll just get dressed and then we can go."

His warm hand wrapped around my upper arm and I climbed out of the bed. "Feeling okay?" The deep timber of his voice made tiny shivers race over my nerve endings.

I could only nod, not trusting my voice when he was this close to me. Thankfully, he released my arm and reached into the bag to pull out a pair of jeans, a white T-shirt, and a pair of flip-flops. "Like I said, it's pretty basic stuff."

"It's perfect," I replied, looking over the soft-looking materials. I don't know why, but emotion clogged my throat. I couldn't remember the last time someone had done anything for me. I hadn't even gotten a gift in years. And even though the clothes were necessities and not really a gift, I doubted he would ever know how much it meant to me.

I cleared my throat and looked up at him. "I'll just get dressed and meet you in the hall."

He nodded. "I'll have the nurse ready your chariot."

"My chariot?"

He shrugged sheepishly. "I thought that sounded better than wheelchair."

I grinned. "Totally better."

Getting dressed proved more difficult than I imagined. My body was stiff and sore. My muscles groaned at just about every move I made, and the bruise on my shoulder screamed at me that it wasn't nearly healed enough to lift my arms and put on a T-shirt.

I tossed down the white cotton and picked up the jeans. Propping myself against the bed, I very slowly stuffed my feet into the pants. Every time the rough material brushed against the sensitive skin of my hands, I winced, but I continued on. I wasn't about to board my chariot with my bum flapping in the wind.

I must have taken a lot longer than I thought because Holt came back through the door a few minutes later. He stopped short when he saw me still not dressed and standing beside the bed.

"I seem to be having some trouble," I admitted.

He strode into the room, his boots moving soundlessly over the cold tile floor. "I should have gotten something easier to put on. I didn't think about the use of your hands being so limited."

I snorted. "Are you kidding? You don't even have to be here right now. This isn't your fault."

He kneeled down in front of me, gently brushing away my arms and grasping the jeans by the waist. He moved slow, inching the jeans up my legs. When they brushed my thighs, he rose upward, his face slowly sliding up the front of me until they met mine. My body jerked slightly when his knuckles brushed against the smooth silkiness of my thigh.

"Sorry," he rasped, his voice a rough whisper as he continued to tug the fabric up around my waist. The jeans were low riders, the waistband skimming my hipbones and dipping below my belly button.

His nimble fingers slid along the top edge, brushing against the fabric and my flat stomach (which was jumping with excitement) until he stopped in the center, just inches above the most feminine place on my body, and gently fastened the button. His Adam's apple bobbed in his throat and his eyes seemed heavy-lidded when he reached for the zipper and slowly, achingly slid it upward.

My knees actually started to shake.

What the hell was wrong with me? I didn't even act like this when I discovered that boys existed and didn't actually have cooties like I thought. I didn't even act like this when the most popular guy in school smiled at me from across the hallway and winked before turning around to hang with his buddies.

Of course, I wasn't fifteen now. And the man standing before me, the man with his touch lingering on my stomach, was not a boy. He was all man. A living, breathing total package.

When his pointer finger trailed toward my belly button, I jumped and stepped back. I was so close to the bed that my legs folded and I ended up falling onto the mattress. My shoulder screamed in protest, and I bit down on my lip to keep from crying out.

"I—uh..." he said, stumbling over his words, his cheeks turning slightly pink.

I pushed up onto one elbow. "Sorry for feeling me up?" I finished for him.

He grinned. "That wasn't feeling you up. When I feel you up, you'll know it."

When *he feels me up...*

I didn't know what to make of that statement, so I stuck my foot in his face. "I need my shoes."

He yanked off the tags from a pair black flip-flops. In the center of the straps was a cluster of sparkly gems. They were pretty, and he slid them onto my feet.

He picked up my shirt and looked at me.

I wasn't wearing a bra.

After my reaction to him pulling my pants up underneath my hospital gown, I was positive if I took off this gown I would embarrass myself. Besides, I didn't know him. I wasn't about to go *Girls Gone Wild* and flash him.

"I'll just wear this."

He frowned. "Are you in that much pain?"

I shook my head. "I'm just sore from lying in this bed for so long. And my shoulder is a little banged up from falling."

"You fell?"

I nodded. "In the chair. I was trying to stand and I knocked myself over."

His eyes darkened to the color of storm clouds. "I wish I had gotten there sooner."

Something inside me softened at the regret in his tone. "I think your timing was perfect." I stood up and gave him a playful shove backward. "But I could have done without being thrown in the pool."

"You sank really fast."

"Ha-ha." I gathered up my items, which consisted of my ruined pajamas and the shirt he brought me, shoved it all in the bag he brought, and then headed to the door. I tried to ignore the draft at my back and the way the oversized gown flapped in the wind.

He made a sound in the back of his throat and I turned, looking over my shoulder at him. "What?"

He was stripping off the slate-colored button-up he was wearing over a navy-blue T-shirt with the letters WFD (Wilmington Fire Department) on the front. "You can't wear that."

"I'm covered," I protested.

"Barely," he muttered and came closer, holding the button-up out like it was a coat and we were at some fancy event where the gentleman always helped the ladies with their evening attire.

He held it low enough that I was able to just slip both my arms inside, successfully managing not to bump my bandaged wrists, and then he slipped it up around me, his hands not touching me once.

Thankfully.

Okay, I was a little disappointed. It seemed my body liked his touch. In fact, my body practically hummed whenever he was around. It was beyond strange.

He made short work of the buttons, closing the shirt up around me in record time (making me think he purposefully took forever on that *one* button on my jeans), and then stepped back to admire his work.

The shirt hung to my knees.

He smirked. "You are tiny."

I stuck out my tongue at him. "You're just huge."

He winked.

Heat flooded my cheeks because suddenly commenting on his size took on a whole new meaning.

Thankfully, the nurse pushed open the door and wheeled in my ride. I sank down into the wheelchair and positioned all my belongings in my lap, taking a moment to mourn the fact that everything I owned fit in a single shopping bag.

Down at the entrance of the hospital, Holt disappeared for a few minutes only to return in a truck that I was pretty sure I would need a ladder to get into.

It was huge. It was also cherry-red with not one spec of dirt on it. The rims on the giant tires were chrome, and I actually caught a reflection of myself in the front tire. The side of the truck said HEMI and by the sound of it, it had two mufflers on the back.

When he came around the hood, he laughed at me and the nurse. "You should see your faces."

"You want me to get in that?" I asked dubiously.

The nurse leaned over the back of my chair and whispered in my ear. "Go for it, honey." I glanced over my shoulder at her, but she was staring at Holt.

I wondered if she was telling me to go for a ride in the truck… or with the man driving it.

Holt held out his hand and gave me a look that dared me not to get up. Of course I had to take the challenge. I might be getting released from the hospital, but I was no wimp. I survived being tied up in a fire and tossed into a pool.

Holt splayed his hands around my waist, once again murmuring about my slight size, and lifted me into the cab of the truck like I weighed nothing more than a bag of Skittles.

Mmm. Skittles sounded good.

"Let me help you with that," he said, pulling the seatbelt around me and clipping it in place over my lap. Then he adjusted it across my chest before pulling back to look at my face.

"You ready?"

It was a simple question.

Yet the weight behind it seemed to catch my breath and make me wary. I don't know what kind of emotion came through my face, but he chuckled and

shut the door to go around and get into the driver's
seat. When he pulled away from the curb, I spoke up.

"You can just take me to the motel that's down
near the library."

The truck jerked to a halt and I went forward.
Holt reached out casually and splayed his hand over
my chest, keeping me from going forward any farther.
Then he snatched his hand back and looked at me.
"Motel?"

My eyes widened at the hardness in his tone. "I
appreciate you telling the doctor you would look out
for me, but you didn't really think I would stay with
you, did you?"

"I gave the doctor my word."

I gaped at him. Was he serious? He couldn't
possibly want me at his house any more than I
wanted to be there. "I won't tell him you took me to a
motel."

"I'm not taking you to a motel," he growled.

"Yes. You are."

He completely ignored the fact that he was
sitting in the center of the road and crossed his arms
over his chest and regarded me with raised eyebrows.
"How do you plan to pay for the room?"

"I have a bank account," I snapped, but then I
realized my bankcards, checkbook, and driver's
license burned in the fire. "Oh."

He smirked.

"Was my car damaged?"

"I don't think so."

I blew out a breath. "I have my library ID for
work in my glove compartment. I can use that at the
bank." Thank God I kept it there. I also kept a twenty
in there with it because once I left my wallet at home

and starved the entire day because I had no money to buy lunch.

"It's after five," he said, pointing at the clock on the dash. "Banks are closed."

I leaned my head back against the seat. It was starting to hurt. "Look. No offense. I am grateful to you for saving my life. For checking on me in the hospital and for bringing me these really cute flip-flops, but I don't know you. I can't just come to your house."

"You're scared of me." He said it like the words left a bad taste in his mouth.

"No." I protested. I really wasn't. He made me feel... safe. But that was the problem. I wasn't safe. Someone tried to kill me. I couldn't just go home with some stranger because I didn't want to be alone.

"Someone tried to kill you."

"I know." I held up my wrist.

"I'm not taking you to a motel."

"It's not your decision."

"I'm the one driving."

"You're stupid!" I yelled.

He laughed. A real laugh that started in his belly and burst out of his chest. I giggled. I just called him stupid like I was twelve.

A car sitting behind the truck beeped their horn loudly, then sped out around us, the driver sticking his very unfriendly finger out the window and waiving it wildly around.

"Well, I guess he told me," Holt said and flashed his teeth.

I giggled some more.

He put the truck in drive and pulled away. His face turned serious. "Do you really have no one?"

I sighed. "I can take care of myself."

"How is it that someone like you ended up all alone?"

His words caused a hollow feeling inside me. It kind of felt like a giant pocket of air that kept expanding until there was nothing left but the pressure of emptiness inside me. "It's a long story."

"I have time."

"I'm tired," I said. I leaned farther into the seat and looked out my window at the passing buildings. The sun was low in the sky and I knew in just a few hours, darkness would blanket the town, covering up all traces of sunlight. I wasn't sure I was ready for the darkness.

The last time I went to sleep in the dark, I woke up tied to a chair in the middle of a raging fire.

"Look. Let me take you to my place tonight. In the morning, I can take you to the bank and to whatever motel you want. It's only one night."

I felt myself beginning to succumb to his words. I knew I would sleep better if he were close by. I tried not to think about that too much because I didn't like it. I really was tired. My body was sore and all I really wanted was to take some pain meds and curl up beneath a blanket. A soft one.

"Fine. I'll stay."

He smiled like a cat that ate a canary.

"But if you try to kill me in my sleep, I will come back as a ghost and make your life a living hell."

He did that immediate brake thing again, using his arm to keep me from flying forward. I let out an exasperated sigh. "You are a terrible driver."

"Katie, look at me."

The command in his voice was undeniable.

I looked up.

He regarded me with somber eyes. "I swear to you I will *never* hurt you."

Deep down I knew it. It was almost like an instinct. Like when you meet someone and right away you know they are a liar. Or that right away they give you the creeps. Well, with Holt—the minute I saw him, I knew. I knew he was a good guy. My subconscious called him a superhero. He wasn't a liar or a creep—I would sense it if he were. Wouldn't I?

You didn't know someone was trying to kill you, an evil voice in the back of my head whispered.

I told it to shut up.

I glanced back at him again. He was rubbing his stubbly chin with his hand, regarding me in a way that showed the doubt in his eyes. He was nervous. It was kind of cute.

"If you slam on the brakes one more time, I'm going to insist on driving."

A slow smile spread over his face. "No women are allowed to drive this truck."

I lifted a single eyebrow. "Is that so?"

"Damn straight."

And just like that, I was going home with a hot fireman stranger.

5

I didn't realize the enormity of going home with him until he pulled in the concrete driveway beside his single-story home. It was a cute place—with a front porch that cried out for rocking chairs and extended the entire length of the front of the home. It was a newer built home, the siding a blue-gray color with wooden shaker-style shutters on each side of the window in a deep-brown shade.

The front door was white, and I knew if it had been my house, the first thing I would have done was paint it to match the shutters.

But this wasn't my house.

My cute little house was no more.

"Everything okay?" Holt asked, turning to face me when I made no move to climb out of the truck.

"I like your house."

"Thanks. I haven't lived here very long. The inside's pretty bare."

"Like a clean slate," I murmured without thinking.

"More like a bachelor pad."

I glanced at him, feeling my lips pull into a half smile.

He didn't say anything else but got out of his monster-sized truck. I opened the door and stared down at the ground hesitantly, thinking about how far up I actually was.

"Going down?" Holt said in a distinguished tone. He held out his hand and I didn't hesitate placing mine inside.

His hand merely cupped mine, so gentle it was like he wasn't holding on to me at all, and his skin felt cool against my heat-burned skin. Then he was taking me by the waist, lifting me down, and setting me gently on the pavement.

He didn't step back but instead stayed in my personal space—invading it, taking it over. He leaned forward, causing me to lean back, and we bent in a gentle arch while he reached in and collected my sad bag of belongings.

Then he straightened and palmed the edge of the door and smiled, still not moving back.

I ducked around him, brushing up against his side as I moved. The brief contact sent a little sizzle of desire through me.

Get a grip, Katie! I told myself, disgusted with my own behavior.

I heard a soft chuckle from behind, and I resisted the urge to turn and glare at him. Did he know the effect he had on me?

"Come on Katie-cat, let's go inside. It's hot out here."

"Do not call me Katie-cat."

"Why not?" he said, glancing over his shoulder while he unlocked the front door.

"Because I'm not twelve."

"Thank God for that," he muttered as the door swung open and a blast of cool air reached out and beckoned me inside. Summers in the south were brutal and today was a scorcher.

"I love air-conditioning," I said as I followed him into the house. I pretended not to hear his last remark. I didn't want to think too closely about what it meant anyway.

"Everyone in the south loves a/c," he said, pushing the door shut behind me.

His home was beautiful. It was a single-story ranch home with an open layout. We were standing by the front door that opened into a fairly large living room. The walls were off-white and the floors were made out of dark hardwood. There were shades covering the windows but no curtains. The shades were white, so it allowed light to get in without disrupting privacy. The only piece of furniture in the living area was a large gray couch and—big shocker—there was a flat screen mounted to the wall.

From my position, I could see directly into the kitchen, which was separated from the living room by a large island with a couple barstools slid underneath. Behind the island, I could make out stainless steel appliances and dark-wood cabinets. There was a space off to the side of the kitchen for a dining table, but there wasn't one there.

Off to our right was a hallway that I assumed led to the bathroom and bedrooms.

"How long have you lived here?" I asked.

"About six months."

I made a noise in the back of my throat—a noise that irritated the already sensitive area. "You've lived here *six* months and only managed to get a couch and a TV?"

He grinned. "I have a bed too."

I rolled my eyes.

He moved into the house, tossing his car keys and cell phone onto the island, and opened the fridge to pull out a bottle of water. He unscrewed the cap and carried it over toward me, extending it. "How's your throat?"

"It's fine, thank you," I said, taking the offered drink and sipping.

"You gonna stand at the door all night?" he asked, going over and flopping onto the couch.

He took up half of it.

Being here suddenly seemed like a bad idea. I guess I hadn't thought about what it would be like to be truly alone with him. At the hospital, someone was always out in the hall. The nurses were always coming in and out, but here… here there was only him and me.

He glanced over the back of the couch, his bright eyes spearing me in the fading light of the room. "You hungry?"

My stomach rumbled. I nodded.

"Pizza?"

I nodded again. "Veggie?"

He made a face. "Please tell me you don't eat nothing but lettuce."

I smiled, the tense muscles in my back relaxing. "No, but I like veggie pizza."

"Sausage too?"

I nodded even though sausage wasn't my favorite.

"Veggie it is!" He must have had the pizza place on speed dial because he had the pizza ordered in five seconds flat.

I decided to stop clinging to the door and moved farther into the room, slipping my flip-flops off and leaving them beside the door.

"So, Freckles," he said when I sat down.

"Freckles?" I interrupted.

"You said I couldn't call ya, Katie-cat."

I shuddered. "I do have a given name, you know."

"I don't want to call you what everyone else calls you."

"You don't?"

"Nope."

"Why?" I asked suspiciously.

"Because I'm special."

"There goes that ego of yours again." I held out my arms wide. "Big," I mouthed.

A few minutes later, the pizza arrived and I was a little shocked at how fast that happened. But when Holt opened the door and greeted the delivery guy by name, I understood. He must eat a lot of pizza.

When the box was open in front of us, the TV volume was turned down low, and napkins were scattered on the couch between us, he shoved half a slice in his mouth and then looked at me. "So, Freckles, who's trying to kill ya?"

I choked a little on the bite as I swallowed, a little shocked at his bluntness. "No one."

He looked at me in disbelief.

"I think it was just a random thing. A burglary gone wrong. The police seem to agree."

"You think someone tying you to a chair and pouring gasoline all over your house was random?"

I set down the pizza, no longer hungry. "Yes, I do. I don't know anyone who would try to kill me."

He regarded me for long moments. "No one?"

"You say that like I'm some criminal with a bunch of mobster friends."

He laughed. "There is no mob in Wilmington."

I leaned in. "You sure about that?" I deadpanned.

His eyes widened a little and I grinned.

"Funny," he said and shoved the rest of the pizza into his mouth.

"May I use your restroom?"

"Make yourself at home," he said and then directed me toward the right room.

I shut myself in the bathroom and studied myself in the mirror. It was just as I thought. I looked like crap. Well, except for my hair, thanks to the nurse. It actually looked good, falling in waves over my shoulders and onto my chest. It actually stayed fairly straight too, the cinnamon-colored, thick strands only taking on a bit of waviness, likely from the time I spent in the hospital bed. My skin was paler than usual, making the practically orange freckles that scattered across my cheeks and nose stand out. My eyes were light colored, blue, but they weren't icy cool like Holt's. They were more grayish, like a stormy sky, and were lined with light-red eyelashes that kind of disappeared against my skin (thank goodness for mascara). My lips were full and peach-colored, on the pale side, and I usually used gloss to give them more pop.

I looked down at Holt's shirt buttoned up over my hospital gown and grinned ruefully. I looked ridiculous. Carefully, I peeled off his shirt and untied the gown from around my neck. It was so large it fell around my bare feet in a puddle. I covered back up with Holt's shirt, glad for once that my breasts weren't large because I didn't have a bra to hold them up. I couldn't help but notice how comfortable the worn fabric of his shirt was against my skin and how it carried the scent of him, which caused me to breathe a little deeper.

I shoved the gown in the trash, hoping I would never have to wear one like it again, and then did my business and left the bathroom. By the time I was back on the couch, I felt weary and my injuries were hurting.

"Everything come out okay?" Holt said when I sat down.

"Did you seriously just ask me that?" I couldn't help but laugh.

"You were gone a long time."

"My hands are burned and so are my wrists!"

That seemed to wipe the humor off his face. I hadn't meant to do that. "Want me to help you with the bandages?"

"No, the nurse did it before you arrived."

"You barely ate," he observed.

I picked up the pizza and took a bite, not because I wanted it, but because he clearly wanted me to. I paused in chewing. Since when did I do things because someone else wanted me too? Uh, never.

I set the pizza back down and scooted into the couch cushions, leaning my head back and trying to get comfortable. I felt homesick. I missed my couch, my favorite blanket, and my house. I knew this was only temporary, that I would have my own place again, but I hated temporary.

Temporary was just a word—a state of being that really just meant nothing was mine. It was like I was borrowing something that didn't belong to me.

I was tired of that.

I wanted permanent.

Some action movie was playing on the flat screen and I turned my attention toward that, trying to distract myself. I was only tired. Tired and upset. A combination that always made me feel slightly grouchy and, tonight, kind of sad.

Tomorrow I would feel better.

Holt snorted at something on the TV and I turned my head to look at him. He was so solid looking—wide shoulders, strong jaw, and rock-hard biceps. The stubble on his face was soft, setting off some of the hardness he projected. His presence was reassuring; somehow he made me feel like everything was going to be okay.

The blurry vision of him stepping through the fire to rescue me arose in my head, and I tried to see more of him, but a memory was just that—a memory. I couldn't really pull more detail out of that moment even though I wanted to. If I were able, I doubt I would notice how good-looking he was in his fireman's gear. If anything, I would notice the way the flames devoured my home.

I closed my eyes, willing myself to stop thinking altogether. I took a few deep breaths and positioned my arms so my wrists wouldn't get squished beneath my body. It didn't take long to drift off into soundless sleep. Every once in a while, the TV would break into my slumber, but I found the sound comforting. It made me feel less alone.

I don't know what time it was when I felt myself being moved. Alarm slammed through me—my instincts thinking someone was somehow taking advantage of me in my sleep. I jerked awake, flinging my arms wide while my body went rigid.

"Everything's fine. You're safe." Holt's voice was a soft rumble beside my ear.

I blinked, looking up. I was in his arms. He was cradling me against him and my cheek brushed against his T-shirt-clad chest. "What are you doing?" I mumbled, my eyes drifting closed again.

"You'll be more comfortable in a bed."

He carried me like I weighed nothing, and his body gave off a delicious heat that my skin just soaked up like a flower on a sunny day. Then he was laying me in a bed with soft sheets and tucking a blanket up around my shoulders.

I could have sworn I felt the brush of his lips at my hairline, but it could have been a dream because just after that brief feeling of contact, deep sleep claimed me completely.

6

Something was burning. I shot up in the center of a very large bed. The first few moments, I sat there disoriented, trying to remember where I was.

I remembered the fire. The hospital. I remembered being carried to bed by Holt.

Something was on fire.

Again.

Acting swiftly, I threw off the covers and jumped down, barely noticing how chilled the wooden floors felt against my feet. I looked for signs of the fire as I rushed out into the hallway, ducking slightly low in case of rising smoke.

A loud piercing beep assaulted the quiet morning and went off with an enthusiasm that could only be produced by a really good battery.

"Holt!" I shrieked, my voice straining to reach the volume I wanted. "Fire! Get out of the house."

My heart was beating so fast I thought it might collapse in my chest. My knees began to shake with adrenaline as I bolted into the living room and rushed toward the front door.

I had to get out.

I did not want to burn.

"Holt!" I screamed again, tearing open the door, preparing to rush out into the yard.

Something caught me around the waist and pulled me back into the house. My feet were lifted off the floor, but they continued to make a running motion, kicking whatever was holding me.

"No, please!" I yelled, trying to squirm free.

"Katie!" Holt said, his voice loud against my ear. "It's me. There is no fire."

I stopped struggling, going limp in his arms. He reached around us and shoved the door closed, spinning around and facing us toward the kitchen.

"I was trying to make you breakfast."

It took a moment for his words and their meaning to sink in. I stared dumbfounded across the room and past the island. There was smoke billowing up from the stove and the window above the sink was wide open.

Bowls and spoons littered the island and there was a carton of eggs sitting out.

He was trying to cook.

He was really bad at it.

I started to laugh.

The kind of laugh that shook my shoulders and bubbled up hysterically. My heart rate was still out of control, and I took in a few breaths between laughs to try and calm it down.

He said something, but I couldn't hear him because the fire alarm was still going off. I had no doubt half the neighborhood was now awake from the sound. He didn't bother to put me down, instead hauling me along with him, where he finally set me down, dragged a chair over near the alarm, and climbed up to remove the battery.

The noise cut off and the kitchen fell silent.

"Well, shit," he said, staring at the battery in his hand.

A giggle escaped me. "Does this always happen when you cook?"

He shrugged. "The only time I ever cook is when it's my turn at the station." His forehead creased and a thoughtful look came over his face. "The guys are never around when it's my night to cook. Now I know why." He snagged a towel off the counter and began waving away the rest of the lingering smoke.

I clicked on the vent fan above the stove. There was a pan with half a melted spatula, something that may or may not have once been eggs, and a muffin tin with half-burned, half-raw muffins (how was that even possible?).

"Well, this looks…" My words faltered, trying to come up with something positive to say.

"Completely inedible?" he finished.

I grinned. "You did all this for me?"

"I figured after a week of hospital food, you might like something good. Apparently you aren't going to find that here."

I had the urge to hug him. I kept my feet planted where they were. "Thank you. No one's ever ruined a pan for me before."

He grinned. "I have cereal. Even I can't mess that up."

I watched as he pulled down a bowl and poured me some, adding milk. He looked so cute when he handed me the bowl that I lifted the spoon and took a bite. "Best cereal I ever had."

"Damn straight."

I carried it over to the counter and sat down. "After we eat, would you mind taking me to my car? I hope it's still drivable."

"What about the keys?"

"I have a security deposit box at the bank. I keep my spare there in case I ever need them."

"Pretty smart."

"I have a few good ideas now and then."

"Contrary to the way it looks, I do too."

"Thank you for trying to make me breakfast. And for the cereal."

He walked over to the stove and picked up the ruined pan. "You died with honor," he said, giving it a mock salute. And then he threw the entire thing into the trashcan.

I laughed. "You could have washed it, you know."

He made a face. "No. Then I might be tempted to use it again."

"I should change my bandages and… uh…" I looked down at his button-up. "My clothes."

I noticed his gaze linger on my legs before he spoke up. "I'll help you with those."

For a minute I thought he was talking about my pants, and the memory of the last time he "helped" me with them crept up on me. Heat suffused my system as my body recalled what his touch felt like and how his fingertips lingered on my skin.

He cleared his throat and my attention jerked back to the present, and I realized he wasn't talking about my pants. He was talking about the bandages.

It was official.

I was turning into a pervert.

I retrieved my sack of belongings from the living room and pulled out a few of the medical supplies the nurse at the hospital gave me and spread them out on the kitchen island. Then I sat down on a stool and began unwrapping one of my wrists.

"Here, let me." His voice was gentle as he ushered my hands away and brought my wrist closer to him. He worked quietly, completely unwrapping the wound and then staring down at it with a somber expression. "How's the pain?"

"Manageable," I said, offering him a smile.

"I should have gotten there sooner," he said to himself.

Was that blame I heard in his tone? I brought my free hand up and covered his arm. "Holt, I'm alive because of you."

"But you still got hurt."

"It would have been a lot worse," I murmured, thinking back to that night. "I thought you were just a hallucination," I confided and he looked up, listening to my words. "I'd been trying desperately to get to my feet, to run toward the back of my house, but my ankles were crossed, it made it hard to stand. When I did manage, I fell over."

He didn't say anything, but he did flip his arm over and slid it down so his fingers could grasp mine.

"I've never been so afraid in my entire life. The heat, it's so intense, you know?" He nodded and I went on. "It was getting really hard to breathe, and I could feel my consciousness slipping away. And then there you were. Stepping through the flames like some kind of superhero."

"Maybe I should get a cape," he quipped.

I laughed lightly. "Maybe. We were lucky the fire hadn't spread to the back door."

"You know I didn't actually walk through the flames. We aren't supposed to do that."

I tilted my head to the side. "It sure looked that way from where I was sitting."

He nodded. "The flames were close. Closer than we would have liked. We were actually told to fall back, to go around the back of the house. But I knew if I left, if I did what they said, you would have died."

The enormity of what he did overwhelmed me. He continued forward even after he was told he shouldn't. He literally risked his own life for mine. I wasn't going to bother telling him it was a reckless choice, that he shouldn't have done it. Because I was glad he did. And I certainly wasn't going to make less of what he did by telling him he was wrong.

"Did you get in trouble?"

His smile was lightning fast. "Nah. The chief loves me."

I bet he did. I couldn't imagine anyone not loving him.

He went back to working on my wrist, applying the creams I was given and rewrapping the wound like he was handling a newborn puppy or something equally as precious.

It hurt, but the pain was overshadowed by his nearness, by the sound of his even breathing, and by the looks of concern those incredible blue eyes bestowed upon me.

"Breathe," he reminded me, pausing in his ministrations.

I hadn't realized I was holding my breath. I took a breath and he went back to work. He probably thought I was holding my breath because of the pain. It wasn't the pain. It was him. He was unlike any man I had ever known. It took a truly strong man to be so gentle. And he was selfless, too, putting my life ahead of his own that night.

Of course, I wasn't about to tell him that.

He flashed me a small smile, almost like he could read my thoughts, and then lifted my other wrist and he began the process all over again.

I glanced over at my cereal, long forgotten and turned to mush.

"You can make another bowl after I'm done," he said, the words rumbling out of his chest as he worked.

"I can just stop on the way to the motel and get something."

His eyes flashed up to mine. "Motel?"

I nodded. "I'll stay at one until I'm able to get another place."

"You can stay here."

"I can't."

"Why not?"

I opened my mouth to give some kind of reply when he demanded, "Do you have a boyfriend?" The anger in his tone was surprising.

"No!"

He fell silent again as he finished up bandaging me. When he was done, he grasped my forearm up above the burns. "Katie, please stay here."

I felt my insides caving. I looked away. If I couldn't see the persuasion in his eyes, I wouldn't be tempted. After all, I did feel safe with him and after everything that happened, feeling safe seemed really important.

He's still a stranger. The sensible voice in my head reminded me.

For once in my entire life, I found myself not wanting to be sensible.

"Holt, I—"

He leaned forward, tugging on the collar of his button-down. "I like seeing you in my shirt."

I liked wearing it. It was like being wrapped in his arms all the time.

He brushed his thumb across the fullness of my lower lip, his pupils dilating a bit on contact. From there, his thumb trailed over my jaw and down my neck, creating a charge of electricity between our skin. His hand tangled into the ends of my hair, and I knew he was going to kiss me.

And I was going to let him.

In fact, I kind of wished he would hurry up already.

Just as his lips descended upon mine, the doorbell rang. I jerked back like I got my hand caught in the forbidden cookie jar. His shoulders slumped and he sighed. "Don't go anywhere," he told me, and then he muttered the entire way to the door about bad timing.

It was kind of endearing.

He pulled open the door and I swear all the heat in the room was instantly sucked out to be replaced by an arctic wind.

"I'm busy," Holt said in a cold tone that I never heard from him before and moved to shut the door on whomever was outside.

"Ha-ha, very funny." A feminine voice came from the other side. "We both know you aren't busy," she said, pushing past him and stepping into the house.

Of course she was stunning. She had ultra-blond hair cut in a shoulder-skimming sleek bob, with not an ounce of frizz in sight. Her make-up was applied impeccably over skin that appeared to never see the harsh southern sun. She was tall and willowy, her movements graceful, and she was wearing short white tennis shorts and a hot-pink fitted polo with a pair of strappy sandals.

Compared to her, I looked like a troll. A short, frizzy troll full of bruises and bandages.

Her gaze landed on me instantly. I stood. "Hi—" I started, but she narrowed her eyes.

"Who the hell are you?"

Oh, I knew her kind. The kind of girl that thought she was queen bee of everything. Even if you were intimidated, you couldn't show it because once someone like her smelled fear, it would all be over.

I lifted my chin. "Who the hell are you?" I countered.

Holt grinned and gave me a wink from over her shoulder. Then in a no-nonsense tone, he said, "This isn't a good time, Taylor."

Taylor was busy taking in an eyeful of my attire—or lack thereof. Her eyes met mine and a spiteful glint came into them. She sauntered across the carpet to stand in front of me, peering down her nose at me (I wasn't about to lift my head and look up to her), and she offered a perfectly manicured hand. "I'm Taylor. Holt's wife."

Shock rippled through my entire body, and it was all I could do to not let my mouth drop open. I looked at Holt, who looked like he swallowed an entire bag of lemons, and said, "You're married?"

He opened his mouth to reply when my attention was drawn away. "Go put on some clothes. I don't fancy seeing you dressed in my husband's shirt."

Oh. My. God.

I was going to die of shame.

I rushed out of the room, toward the bedroom where I hurried to find my jeans and shirt. It hurt to pull on the clothes, but I barely noticed. My mind was too busy swimming with thoughts.

How could I be so stupid? What kind of guy brings home other women and lets them sleep in their clothes when they have a wife? I was going to let him kiss me!

This was exactly why I never bothered to get close to people. This was exactly why I preferred taking care of myself.

Once my clothes were on, I rushed from the room—not even paying attention to the raised voices—grabbed my pathetic plastic sack, and then ran out onto the porch.

The door didn't even close behind me before Holt was calling for me to stop.

I did, but only because he was my ride.

"I need my car," I told him, not bothering to turn around.

I felt him behind me. His closeness had my body tingling, and I pushed it away, trying to ignore the feeling. He stepped around me, stopping so close my toes almost touched his.

"She's not my wife," he said, his voice for my ears only.

"So she's delusional?"

"No, she's just a bitch."

That had my head snapping up to see him. He grinned ruefully and shrugged.

I didn't say anything. I just waited for whatever else he wanted to say so we could go.

He sighed. "She's my *ex*-wife. Emphasis on the ex."

"You were married to that?" I asked skeptically.

"Unfortunately. We were high school sweethearts. She grew out of being a sweetheart."

I snorted.

"How long ago did you get divorced?"

He hesitated, which made me think I probably wasn't going to like his answer. "It was final six months ago."

That explained the new house and lack of furnishings.

"But we've been separated for over a year," he quickly added.

"What's she doing here?" I asked, looking back to the porch where she was watching us.

"She likes to show up from time to time and make me miserable."

"Why did you get divorced?" I asked suspiciously.

"Taylor likes money. I don't make enough."

Disgust had me wrinkling my nose. "You're kidding."

The way his jaw worked made me realize he wasn't, and he wasn't exactly happy to admit someone found him… lacking.

"You're right," I said as a strange protective feeling came over me. "She is a bitch. She's stupid too."

Relief flooded his eyes. "You believe me?"

"Yeah, I do." It still didn't change the fact it was time for me to go. He reached out to take my bag. I pulled it back. "I really do want to get my car."

He shook his head grimly. "I'll just get my keys."

He jogged into the house, retrieved his keys, then shut and locked the door while Taylor stood by looking very smug. I heard the automatic locks inside the truck and stepped forward to climb inside.

But then I stopped.

I turned around and waved my fingers at Taylor. "Don't worry, I'm nothing to be jealous of. I'm just using Holt for sex. He's *so* good in bed."

Her mouth dropped open.

I climbed in the truck.

Holt was still laughing when he fired up the engine and backed out of the driveway. Since her car was parked right behind his, he had to swerve wide and drive on the lawn before pulling out onto the street and driving away.

Taylor just stood there and watched.

"You're a little feisty, aren't you?" he said, giving me an approving stare.

"I am a redhead."

We didn't talk after that. I only broke the silence to tell him where my bank was. He waited outside when I went in to get my key. Thankfully, one of the tellers there recognized me and opened the box after I explained my situation and showed her my bandages. Once I had the key, I thanked her profusely and promised to come with my library ID so I could get new account cards and make a withdrawal from my account.

The entire way to my house, my stomach was in knots. I wasn't sure I wanted to see what was left of my beloved home. I knew it wasn't going to be pretty, and I tried to prepare myself for the reality I was about to face.

Up until now, part of this felt like a bad dream. If I wasn't sitting here with Holt and feeling the constant nagging of painful burns, I might have been able to convince myself I'd imagined the whole thing.

But then he turned onto my street.

You couldn't deny what stared you directly in the face.

What was once a sunny yellow two-story home with bright-pink rosebushes lining the front and potted plants decorating the porch now looked like something out of a horror movie.

Some of the structure was partly standing. The remaining timbers were black and brittle looking. The roof had long since caved in and a few scorched shingles littered the ashy covered grass. Most of the walls had fallen down; only two outside walls still partly remained. The concrete steps that once led to the front door were all blackened with fire marks and soot. All the flowerpots that held colorful annuals were shattered. Pieces of clay and dirt lined the once swept clean walkway.

It looked so out of place sitting there in the center of the small, tucked away neighborhood amongst the cheerful houses and blooming flowers. It was almost as if my house resided in a completely different universe than those on each side. Like hell had opened up some sort of portal of destruction, unleashed its wrath on only my little slice of the country, and then vanished, leaving behind the skeletal remains of what was once a peaceful life.

I looked past the house directly into the small backyard, taken up mostly by the kidney shaped pool. Debris floated in the water, pieces of my life that were too ruined to identify. And beside it... sitting on the concrete just beside the pool...

Was a chair.

My chair.

The one I was tied to.

In fact, a length of rope still lay coiled beneath it.

I felt as if I were in a vacuum and the memories of my attempted murder were trying to suck me up where all I could do was relive them over and over again.

"I should have had that moved," Holt said, coming up just behind me to stand.

I tore my gaze away from the chair, away from the rope that tried to hold me hostage. "The police told me they would let me know when the house was clear, and I could search it for anything that might have survived," I told him as a breeze ruffled my hair. It also drifted the still lingering scent of melted plastic and burned timber toward us. "But by the looks of things, there isn't going to be anything left to save."

"I'm sorry," he said quietly, his fingers brushing across mine.

I looked over my shoulder at him. "It's okay. Just about everything can be replaced."

"Just about?" he asked curiously.

I nodded. "There was one thing that could never be replaced." The realization caused an ache to erupt inside me. I felt a loss that I didn't think I would ever have to feel again. How would I survive something like that twice?

I didn't realize that I swayed on my feet until a strong arm wrapped around my waist and offered some support.

I leaned on him for a few seconds and then pulled away. "Thank you for the ride. For everything."

"You really need to stop thanking me." His lip tilted up in the corner.

I pulled the key out of my pocket and hugged the bag against my chest, putting a barrier between us. "Well, I have a lot to do," I began, not really knowing what to say.

"You're sure you won't stay at my place?"

I nodded. "I'm sure."

Now more than ever I wanted to be alone. I wanted some time to think—to absorb what had happened. I needed to regroup and make a plan. Once I had a plan, I would feel more in control.

I glanced back at the gaping hole that was my home.

I needed to get out of here. Being here, seeing this, was not helping. It was making everything worse.

"I have to go," I told him.

He frowned, watching me like I was on the verge of some mental breakdown.

Maybe I was.

I didn't bother to try and say anything else. It didn't matter what I said anyway. It would all come out awkward. I walked to my car, which was covered in soot and ash, and climbed inside. I turned the key, letting out a breath when the engine roared to life. I cranked the air and then leaned over, opening the glove compartment, smiling a little when my ID and a twenty spilled out.

I had an ID.

I had a twenty.

I had my car.

It was a start.

I pulled out of the driveway and pointed my car away from the destruction. The hollow feeling in my chest, the ache deep in my bones didn't lessen as I drove away.

Even still, I didn't look back.

7

I chose a locally owned motel—not one of the chain hotels in the area. This one was small and less crowded looking. Plus the rates here were a lot less than the other places I looked. Yes, I had money in savings—but very little. Everything I'd saved as a teenager had gone into the purchase of my little house and all the furnishings inside.

I knew I would get the bulk of it back (thank goodness for insurance), but it would take a while, and until then I was going to have to be very careful about how much money I spent.

After I paid for a single room, I drove my car down the parking lot. It was a one-story motel made entirely of brick, and all the rooms sat connected together in a row. All the doors were red, and I drove past the line of them toward the end unit where I parked my car.

I still hadn't been shopping, so I had nothing to bring inside but my little bag of ruined pajamas and the bandages the nurse gave me at the hospital. The inside of the room was very basic. A twin-sized bed sat in the center of the room with a dark-blue quilt covering the top. The carpet was also dark blue—the kind that wasn't really there for comfort but necessity. There was a tall wooden dresser against the wall and the television sat on top of it. There were a couple of ocean prints hanging on the white walls and heavy blue draperies hanging on the window beside the door. Because this was an end unit, I got the luxury (if you could call it that) of having an extra window on the far right wall with the same heavy drapery.

There was a small bathroom with a single sink, toilet, and shower. The shower curtain was white and so were the scratchy-looking towels.

It wasn't my idea of home, but it would do for a while.

I spent the next two days dealing with the insurance company, the bank, the driver's license office, and shopping at Target for some new things to wear. I managed to keep my job and get the weekend off, needing to report back to work on Monday morning.

I didn't sleep well in the little motel room. The bed was uncomfortable and I kept waking up flushed with sweat and feeling my heart pound, only to not remember what I was dreaming about.

When darkness covered the sky on the second night, my stomach began to churn with nerves.

I wondered what Holt was doing, if he was at work. Part of me wanted to see him, to be comforted by his presence. But it wasn't his responsibility to comfort me. He'd already done enough for me— saving my life and giving me somewhere to stay my first night out of the hospital.

I told myself the reason I kept thinking about him was because he saved me. He literally walked through fire to carry me to safety. If it hadn't been for him, I wouldn't be here at all. I was somehow bonded to him. I felt like he was literally my lifeline. I supposed it was natural and would fade over time, hopefully sooner rather than later. I kept looking at the phone, like I wanted to call him to hear his voice, but I knew I shouldn't.

I settled for taking a quick shower instead—skipping washing my hair (too much wrist involvement)—and then changing my bandages. The burns didn't seem as bad as before—they still hurt; it was just more bearable.

After showering, I pulled on a pair of sleep shorts and a tank top from one of the shopping bags and dressed carefully. My muscles felt a lot better today, as well as the bruise on my shoulder, finally a fading yellow color.

Everything was going to be okay. My body was healing. I still had a job. I would get the insurance money, and I could buy a new house. Soon, everything would be back to normal.

I watched reruns of *Friends* on the TV until my eyes wouldn't stay open anymore, and I shut it off and snuggled down in the covers, falling asleep quickly.

But I didn't stay asleep very long.

I was awakened by the sound of shattering glass.

As my eyes sprang open, I heard a hard thud on the floor a few feet from the bed. I jolted up immediately, trying to focus my sleep-heavy eyes.

Something orange caught my eye, and then a familiar scent wafted into my nose.

Pure panic burst inside me. It was so strong that I felt dizzy, and I sat there battling it, trying to take control. I leapt to my feet and stared across the room at the bottle that had been thrown through the window.

It was on fire.

I took a single step closer, peering down at the glass.

It was a jar of some kind. It had a rag stuffed halfway into it. The exposed ends were blazing, catching the floor around it on fire as well. I grabbed a pillow off the bed, thinking I could smother it, and stepped closer, trying to shut down the panic that was still trying to take control of my body and mind.

When I was a few feet from jar, it exploded. It made a sharp pop and then glass flew everywhere. I screamed, shielding myself with the pillow, and jumped back, hitting the corner of the bed and falling backward. My head bounced off the floor, and the pillow landed on top of my face.

I lay there sprawled out, trying to catch my breath. The telltale whoosh had me scurrying off the floor and tossing the pillow aside. The curtains were on fire. In fact, most of that side of the room was on fire. The jar must have been filled with some kind of gasoline. When it exploded, fire burst everywhere.

Knowing I couldn't put out the fire, I ran toward the door, fumbling with the chain and then yanking the handle.

The door wouldn't budge.

I tried again.

Nothing.

There was something blocking the exit.

I rushed toward the window beside the door and yanked open the curtains, trying to see what was in the way.

The window was blocked too.

I glanced back at the raging fire. It consumed that side of the room like a hungry wolf, and I knew soon it would be spreading toward me.

Smoke was beginning to cloud the room, making it harder to breathe. I rushed to the nightstand and dialed 9-1-1.

I waited anxiously for the operator to come onto the line.

There was no ringing. No operator.

There was no dial tone.

No help.

Someone cut the phone line.

With an anguished cry, I dropped the receiver and looked around wildly for something—anything that would help me.

I ended up throwing myself against the door, banging on the wood and screaming for help. Surely someone in another room would hear me. Surely someone would help.

Except I was the only car in the parking lot when I got back.

The front desk. Someone was always there. Hopefully they would smell the fire and come to investigate.

I kept screaming, yelling for help. The effort robbed me of the oxygen I needed, and a familiar pressure began to build in my chest.

It was the same feeling from the night I almost died.

Not again.

Thinking fast, I grabbed up the lamp, yanking the cord out of the wall, and went to the window, smashing the lamp into the glass. It cracked but didn't shatter. I hit the glass again; this time a large shard fell to the floor and burst at my feet.

I ignored the fresh, stinging cuts on my feet as I reached my hand out the broken glass and tried to shove away whatever was there. It was really heavy. It didn't even budge.

I started to cry.

I was trapped in here with a blazing fire. I had moments—maybe seconds left to live. I was going to die because I didn't know how to get out.

Just then I heard a loud crashing sound.

Someone was outside!

I started to scream anew, putting my face up to the broken glass and yelling as loud as I could.

The door to the room splintered and burst in, fragments of wood going everywhere.

"Katie!" someone roared.

"Holt!" I cried, jerking away from the window and rushing toward the door.

Flames were dangerously close now, eating up part of the doorframe and the carpet below. The rush of oxygen that came into the room with the opening of the door seemed to fuel the flames even more, and they burst forward in a great rush, completely overtaking the exit.

The bulky outline of Holt was suddenly concealed by flames.

I screamed his name again. Fear that he was burned turned my knees to Jell-O. I heard him cuss and call for me again, and then there was another crash and whatever was sitting in front of the window was gone.

Holt was there punching through the broken glass and reaching a bloodied arm through the opening.

"Come on!" he yelled.

I rushed to the window, pausing to grab my few shopping bags nearby and throwing them out the opening (hey, it was all I had to my name. I wasn't about to let it be destroyed). Holt shoved them away and reached for me as I flung myself out the opening.

And then Holt was there, grabbing me beneath my arms and towing me over the broken vending machines that lay damaged in front of my room and across the parking lot toward his truck, which was haphazardly parked in the center of the empty lot. I couldn't stop coughing. They were deep, menacing coughs that made it hard to walk, and I stumbled onto my knees.

I would have fallen, but he caught me, swinging me up and rushing the rest of the way behind his truck.

I heard more shattering glass and the groan of wood as he sat me down on the hard asphalt and leaned over me.

"I leave you alone for two days," he shouted, shoving his hands through his hair. "What the hell happened!"

He was bleeding. Dark rivulets of blood trailed down his arm and dripped off his elbows onto the ground below. Slowly, I slid down the side of his truck until I was sitting on the ground, still grasping for breath.

"Katie!" he yelled, gripping my shoulder and leaning in to look into my eyes. "Stay with me."

The distant sound of sirens filled the air, and I knew within minutes the place would be swarming with police officers and firefighters. It was minutes I wouldn't have had. If Holt hadn't gotten here when he did, I would likely be dead right now.

That had me looking up.

"What are you doing here?" I asked.

"I came by to check on you. I was worried."

"How did you know where I was?" I said, suspicion leaking into my tone.

He crouched down in front of me, my feet between his legs. "I saw your car in the lot," he explained. "I knew you worked at the library nearby, so I thought you might pick somewhere close to stay."

My shoulders sagged.

He put a hand under my chin and lifted my face. "Look at me," he demanded.

I looked up.

"Do you think this was me?"

"No," I said, ashamed of the catch in my voice. I really didn't think he did this, but I was scared and I was so very tired.

"Can I touch you?" he asked, his voice calm.

I looked up, surprised that he didn't sound angry. I nodded.

He yanked me forward, folding his arms around me and standing up, bringing me with him. My feet touched the ground, but they didn't support me. His arms, his body kept me up. He wrapped himself around me like I was a hand and he was a glove. I clung to the front of his shirt, praying he wouldn't let me go. When his grip tightened, I sighed in relief. His clean scent encompassed me, pushing away some of the smoke, and tears prickled my eyes.

When the emergency trucks swerved into the lot, my muscles tensed at the thought he would release me, that he would push me away and deal with the fire.

But he didn't.

He didn't let go. Not once.

Even when some of the men he must work with came running up—addressing him by his last name and exclaiming over what happened.

He spoke calmly over my head, telling them everything he knew and telling them I wasn't ready to talk. He didn't seem embarrassed to be holding me so close in the center of a parking lot. He didn't act like being seen in a vulnerable position like this wounded his pride at all.

He just stood there in the center of chaos with flames blazing, water spraying, and the shouts of responders all around, and he was completely still.

He was the anchor to my drifting boat. The roots to my growing tree. Without him, I surely would have floated away into some kind of unreachable place within the confines of my brain.

No matter how much I wanted to deny it.

Not matter how much I could say it wasn't true.

There was no getting around it.

This wasn't an accident.

Someone was trying to kill me.

8

The first light of day peeked through the sky when I stepped out of the police station after several hours of questioning. Even after the hours of invasive questions, I knew no one had any clue what was going on. The fact was I didn't have anyone in my life. There was literally no one. And that meant whoever was doing this had motives I didn't know about. Motives I didn't understand.

The police couldn't offer much comfort. They only assured me they would be investigating and warned me to be very careful in my daily life.

Gosh, really?

I was muttering to myself, trying to decide what to do next, when I looked up.

His truck was parked at the curb.

He was leaning against the door, looking smoky and rumpled. His arms were crossed over his chest and he watched me with a heavy stare.

"Holt?" I said, stepping forward. "I thought they released you a couple hours ago."

He pushed away from the truck. "I've been waiting for you." He opened the passenger door and motioned for me to get in.

I noticed my bags sitting on seat. "Is that my stuff?"

He nodded. "It reeks of smoke. You can wash it at home."

"Home?"

"My place."

I opened my mouth to protest, but then I closed it again. I was shaken up. I had nowhere to go, my car was still sitting at the motel, seized for possible evidence, and I didn't want to be alone. If he was offering me a place to stay, then I was going to accept it.

I climbed into the truck and turned to face him. "Good girl," he said.

Before he could slam the door, I caught it with my foot and glared at him. "Good girl?" I mocked. "Do I look like a dog to you?"

He smirked. "No, Freckles, you definitely do not."

I crossed my arms across my chest and glared at him.

He sighed. "Give a guy a break. I'm tired."

"Me too," I said, dropping my attitude.

After he settled behind the wheel, he lifted a pink drink in a clear cup out of the cup holder in the center console. I hadn't even noticed it was there. He extended it to me and I took it.

"What's this?"

"A strawberry smoothie. I figured your throat is probably sore."

It was sore. And it felt very dry. I took a sip of the drink and sighed as the fruity sweetness exploded on my tongue. It's thick and smooth texture slid down my throat with ease. "Thank you," I told him, the words falling flat to my own ears. They just didn't seem to be enough for everything he'd done for me.

He motioned to a white paper sack on the seat beside him and said, "I got you a blueberry muffin, too."

"You didn't get anything?"

"I already ate it."

I sipped the smoothie while he drove, my body feeling boneless against the seat. I was so incredibly tired. The adrenaline that surged through me earlier that night had long ago been used, and it left me feeling drained and empty.

"The medics said you looked okay," Holt said, watching me out of the corner of his eye.

I nodded. "I'm fine."

He lapsed into silence and we said nothing else until we were inside his house and he was handing me a towel for my shower.

"Your hand," I said, noting the raw-looking scrapes and cuts on his knuckles and fingers.

Flashbacks of him punching in the broken window at the motel rushed my brain. I gasped, and the towel in my hand fell to the ground and covered my feet. "Where else are you hurt?"

He shook his head. "I'm not."

I grabbed his hand and brought it back up, studying the damage done to his skin. Lightly, I traced my finger along the edge of one of the more jagged cuts. "They need bandaged," I murmured.

He shook his head. "Bandaging cuts like these on a hand is practically useless. The bandages would just fall off."

"I don't know what to say." My voice was raspy.

"You don't have to say anything. The medics already cleaned and took care of these."

"No," I said, still holding on to his hand. "I don't know how to thank you for saving my life. Again."

"Stop thanking me," he ground out.

"I have to," I said, looking straight into his eyes. "If you hadn't been there…" My sentence trailed away. We both knew what would've happened.

"But I was," he said softly.

"About that…" I began, wetting my lips. "Why were you there?"

"I needed to talk to you about something."

"What?"

He withdrew his hand, reaching into the back pocket of his jeans and pulling out a folded piece of paper. "About this."

It was a plain white piece of paper, the kind that anyone would use in a printer. I unfolded it, noticing there was some kind of writing on the inside. When I got to the last fold, I glanced up at Holt who was wearing a very grim expression. Clearly, whatever this was wasn't good.

I pulled it open and stared down, my brain not really comprehending what it saw. I had to read the line over three times before I really got what it was saying.

My stomach clenched.

My hands trembled slightly.

You should have let her die.

"Where did you get this?" I finally asked.

"It was on my truck when I left work earlier tonight."

The paper fluttered to the floor slowly, joining the towel by my feet. "So you got this before the fire tonight?"

"Yes. It's the reason I came looking for you."

"You didn't say that."

"I figured you were dealing with enough at the moment."

"Did you tell the police?"

He shook his head slowly.

"But why?"

"I wanted to talk to you first. See if you knew what it meant."

"It means someone wants me dead!" I shouted. My voice seemed to echo through the hallway.

"You're not going to die," he growled.

"I shouldn't have come here," I said, looking frantically around. "I need to go." I spun around to rush into the living room, but the towel was tangled around my feet and I tripped, falling toward the floor.

Holt caught me around the waist, pulling me back so I was up against the solid wall of his body. The heat of him was delicious and it radiated around my fear-chilled body. "You're not going anywhere," he rumbled in my ear.

I struggled against him, but it was stupid. He outweighed me by a hundred pounds, easily, and was likely a foot taller than me. If he didn't want to let me go, then I was pretty much stuck in his embrace. I slumped against him. "I'm putting you in danger by being here."

"You're in more danger when I'm not around."

I couldn't stop my snort. "There goes that ego of yours again."

His chuckle vibrated my ear. Chill bumps raced over my scalp. "All I'm saying is that clearly this guy is a pyro. My job is fire. You're better off here than alone."

"But what about you?"

"You let me worry about me."

I tried to wiggle out of his embrace so I could look at him. He only loosened his hold enough to allow me to spin in his arms. I had to tip my head back so I could stare up at him. "Do you have a death wish?"

"I'm not going to die. Especially since life just got a hell of a lot more interesting." His fingers flexed against my hip.

"But—" I protested, but he cut me off.

"It's obvious I'm already in his sights. He thinks we're connected. You not being here isn't going to change that."

I couldn't argue with that because it was true. After all, he didn't receive the letter until after I checked into a motel.

"Why are you helping me?" It was something I just couldn't understand.

His body shifted, I swear coming into even more contact with mine than it already was. He brought up his free hand and brushed back my hair, pushing it so it fell behind my shoulder. "It's my job to protect people."

"Is it your job to bring them home, too?" I felt a little breathless. Just beneath my ribs my heart fluttered wildly. It felt like there was a little bird inside me, flapping its wings, trying to fly.

"That's just a perk of the job." He smirked.

"So you do this often?" I said, feeling slightly bruised.

"Never."

"Then why me?"

He took a few steps, backing me up so I was pinned between him and the wall. From this angle, the hall light fell behind him so his face was in the shadows. But even still, the lightness of his eyes pierced me like a crack of thunder in a storm.

"I don't know."

I wasn't expecting those words. In fact, I barely heard them over the thundering of the blood in my veins. His nearness affected me in ways I didn't understand. I felt hot yet cold. Nervous but bold. Part of me wanted to rush away and the other part of me yearned to arch closer, to slide my hands up the hem of his shirt and run my fingers across the wide expanse of his bare back.

"That's not a very good reason to get mixed up with a girl on the run from a killer."

He cocked his head to the side. "No?"

I shook my head.

"How about this?" he said, leaning down so his lips brushed my jaw. The stubble on his face tickled my chin. "Because even in the center of a blazing fire, my body reacted to you. Because seeing you so small and helpless in a hospital bed twisted my guts. Because the day I walked into your room and those stormy gray eyes landed on mine, I felt like there was something tethering us together. Or maybe it was because of the way you sighed and leaned into my chest the night I carried you to my bed. Your scent still lingers on my sheets, Katie."

Oh my.

I bit my lip. No one had ever said anything like that to me, ever.

He groaned, staring at my mouth. "That drives me crazy."

I released my lip.

"Kiss me, Katie."

My gaze fell to his lips. He was mere inches away; my body was fitted between his legs and against him in a way that left little to the imagination.

I hadn't kissed someone in a long time. I usually found it useless because even if the kiss turned out to be good, it wouldn't matter. I couldn't get attached to someone. I didn't want the pain of saying good-bye.

But I was tempted.

His lips were like a really sinful slice of chocolate cake. You knew if you ate it, you would hate yourself in the morning, but the call of that chocolate was so utterly strong you had to take a bite.

I gazed again at his lips, still inches from mine. He was watching me, watching me debate, watching me try to resist. He didn't try to sway me; he didn't try to make the first move. He just held himself there, as still as a statue, and waited.

Tentatively, I leaned forward, keeping my eyes open, and brushed my lips over his. It was a brief kiss but a full one, and when I pulled back a little, part of my bottom lip seemed to take longer to pull away than the rest of me. It was like it wanted to stay, like it finally knew where it belonged.

I whispered his name as my eyes fluttered closed and his arm slid around my waist, pulling me fully against him. His mouth crashed down on mine, his soft, full lips slanting over me in a way that left no room for thought. A buzzing sound filled my head, the only thing I heard as passion built inside me. He nipped at my bottom lip with his teeth and then sucked it into his mouth, gently massaging it with his tongue. Heat swirled in my center, and I became bolder to release my tongue, letting it mingle with his, brushing them against each other over and over again.

My hands slid up his chest and wound around his neck, trying to pull him down farther, wanting him closer to me.

He slid his knee between my legs and lifted, my back sliding up the wall and my feet leaving the ground. The pressure of his hard leg pressed against my core caused a small purr to rip from my throat.

My thighs clenched around him and he shifted, sliding me even closer, so I could feel the evidence of his desire pressed against my middle. Pressure in my lower half began to build. My body began to long for something more, for some kind of release.

He tore his mouth away, leaning his forehead against the wall beside me. I kept my arms looped around his neck as I pulled in deep gulps of air as I tried to ignore the craving of my lower half.

"Damn, Freckles," he rasped.

Damn, indeed.

Slowly he lowered his leg and me to the ground, and after a few long moments, he stepped back, allowing enough space for me to squeeze by.

Before I could disappear completely into the bathroom, he caught my arm and pulled me back around as he leaned forward and pressed a gentle kiss to my hairline. "If you need anything, just yell."

He handed me the towel and then left me standing in the hall.

In the bathroom, I closed the door and then sagged against it. In a matter of moments, he managed to make me feel a whole host of emotions—fear, humor, lust. But it wasn't any of those that caused me to stand here and realize I was in deep.

It was that last kiss.

The one he pressed to my forehead.

Because a guy who only thought about passion, a guy who only thought about satisfying a need, didn't display that kind of tenderness.

And that kiss was nothing if not tender.

It may have also been my undoing.

9

Beads of sweat gathered on my skin and created a slick sheen of moisture over the surface of my body. The heat was unbearable—intense and thick. Everywhere I turned there was more. There was no escape; there was no relief.

I heard the sound of shattering glass, the angry rush of flames, and I tried to run. Glass shards cut into my feet, making me cry out, but I kept moving, throwing my arms up to shield my face from the burn.

Through my makeshift shield, I spied the door and yanked the handle, trying to pull it open. The metal of the knob scorched my skin, and I cried out, falling backward onto the debris-ridden floor.

I was back in the motel room.

Trapped.

Fire drew closer, devouring everything in its path, promising destruction, promising death.

I pushed up off the floor and banged on the door, screaming for help. I moved toward the window, but it was gone. The only way out was the door... the door that was now consumed by fire.

I backed away… farther into the room, farther into the flames, and the scent of burned flesh and human hair began to fill the space around me.

I screamed.

"Dammit, Katie!" someone yelled. "Wake up!"

His voice broke through the nightmare and my body went completely rigid against the sweat-drenched sheets.

I blinked away the vision of red and orange, letting the darkness of the room surround me. I would take darkness over fire any day.

The mattress dipped slightly on my one side, and I turned my head to find Holt watching me. His bare chest practically glowed in the darkness. "I was having a nightmare," I said, really reassuring myself more than speaking to him.

"I figured that out," he replied dryly. "I thought you were being murdered back here by the way you screamed."

"I'm sorry. I didn't mean to wake you."

A thick strand of damp hair clung to my cheek and he reached out to brush it away. "Wanna talk about it?"

I shook my head. Dreaming it was bad enough.

I sat up, pushing away the sheets tangled around my legs. The scent of smoke seemed to cling to me, reminding me once again of everything I was trying to forget.

I pulled at the tank top I was wearing; it was sticking to my skin. Holt went across the room to the closet and returned with a light-colored T-shirt. "Here. You can put this on if you want."

"Thank you," I said. I wanted these smoke-ridden, sweaty clothes off me, and since all my clothes smelled, this shirt was a lot better than anything I had.

He didn't say anything else, just quietly left the room. I hurried to change, throwing my PJs across the room and into a darkened corner. I'd deal with them later.

A glance at the clock on the nightstand told me I still had several hours until morning, and I knew I was in for a long night. I wasn't quite ready to get back in bed, and my throat felt dry, so I left the bedroom and padded into the kitchen for a bottle of cool water.

On my way back through the living room, I glanced at the couch and froze. Holt was lying there with a blanket tossed over his legs.

"You're sleeping on the couch?" I said, surprise lacing my tone.

"I figured it was too soon to climb into bed with you," he drawled.

A warm flush spread over my limbs. The idea of sharing a bed with him... of being tangled up in his arms and legs... was entirely too appealing. "I'm an idiot."

He chuckled. "And why is that?"

Because I should have realized that he only had one bed in this house and I was hogging it. He did say my scent was on *his* sheets. Geez, how slow on the uptake was I? "I should be the one sleeping out here."

"No." It sounded like a command.

"Yes."

He moved so fast I barely saw him, and then he was towering over me, my eyes left to stare at the very wide expanse of his chiseled chest. "What kind of a man do you think I am?" he drawled.

"What?" I said, not really listening to his words. His body was the ultimate distraction.

"Do you really think I would let someone—a girl—who was just released from the hospital, still bruised and burned, sleep on my couch?"

"I'm sure I would be more comfortable there than you would be."

"Go back to bed, Katie." He crossed his arms over his chest.

"And if I don't?" I challenged. I didn't really care for the overbearing type.

"If you don't, I'm going to rip my shirt off you right here and do things to your body that will echo through your limbs long after I stop touching you."

I took a sip of the chilled water, thinking it would clear my head of the images he just filled it with.

It didn't help.

Part of me was very tempted to see if he would follow through on his words. The other part of me wanted to run away.

He leaned down toward my face. "What's it gonna be, Freckles?"

Like a big fat chicken, I turned and fled into the safety of his bedroom. I jumped onto the mattress like there was something hiding beneath it, waiting to snatch me away. Then I sat in the center of the massive bed and tried to calm the tingle of excitement that coursed through me.

As I buried my head into one of the fluffy pillows and squeezed my eyes shut, I could have sworn his laughter echoed through the darkness.

*   *   *

He was sitting at the kitchen island, eating a bowl of cereal, when I entered the kitchen the next morning. I was relieved to see he was wearing a shirt. Instead of dealing with a pair of jeans or shorts, I opted instead for a simple T-shirt dress in navy blue. I'd wanted to braid my hair but didn't feel like aggravating my wrists, so I left it down to fall halfway down my back.

My eyes about fell out of my head when I saw the size of Holt's cereal bowl—if you could even call it that. It looked more like a bucket and a shovel.

"Holy cow," I observed. "Do you eat an entire box of cereal every morning?"

"Nah," he scoffed, shoving a huge bite into his mouth. "Just half a box." The crunching of his chewing echoed through the room. "I don't have any coffee, but we can go get some," he said around another entirely too large mouthful.

I made a face. "I don't drink coffee."

He grunted. "Me either."

"We must be the only two people on the planet," I mused as I scrounged around his cabinets for a normal-sized bowl and spoon.

When I turned from the counter with an actual portion of cereal in hand, I noticed the paper at his elbow. It was the note. From my biggest fan.

"We should take that to the police."

Holt nodded. "We need to talk."

I sat down beside him, eyeing the note like it was strapped to some kind of bomb ready to detonate at any second.

"You really have no idea who this could be?" he asked.

I shook my head. "I really don't."

"Well, if you ask me, you sure pissed someone off because he seems awfully motivated to burn you to a crisp."

"You keep saying 'he,'" I pointed out.

He shrugged. "It could be a woman."

It could be. But it really didn't feel like it. It seemed if a woman were going to kill me, she would just grab a gun and be done with it. This person seemed to like to play with their prey before they killed it.

"Maybe one of your friends got mixed up in something and dragged you into it without you realizing it."

I stirred my cereal around as he threw out guesses.

"Or maybe it's an ex-boyfriend? An ex-husband?"

I sighed. "No."

"I think you should at least consider the possibility—" he began.

My spoon clattered against the bowl and I pushed away from the counter. "I haven't had a boyfriend in years. And even then, it was no one that mattered."

"Dates gone bad?"

I shook my head.

"You can't really expect me to believe you don't date?" He scoffed.

"I don't," I said flat. "Up until this point, I've lived a very uneventful life."

"What about work?" he asked slowly.

"I'm a librarian. Most of my coworkers are books."

He frowned. "What about the ones who aren't books?"

"One is an elderly lady and the other is an intern. My director doesn't work at my library branch but has a different office. I barely see her."

"Do the police have any leads?"

"Up until last night, they thought my house fire was some kind of random act of violence. I don't think they've had enough time to get any leads."

"So what are they doing?" He made a frustrated sound and ran a hand through his hair.

"I'm sure they're investigating. They just told me to be careful and report anything strange immediately. Which is exactly why we need to take that note to the station."

He looked frustrated and angry.

"Look, this isn't your problem. I'm grateful for everything you've done."

"Don't even suggest that you leave again," he growled.

"I'm not your responsibility!" I said, throwing my hands into the air.

He caught me around the middle, yanking me off the barstool and causing me to stumble into his lap. His hand cradled the back of my head and he stared down at me with angry eyes. His chest was heaving and with every sharp intake of breath, his firm body brushed against my chest. My body didn't seem to notice his anger and only cared about his nearness because my nipples drew into rock hard buds, aching instantly for just one more touch.

I felt breathless, shocked, and excited all at once. Shocked at his display of anger, breathless by my body's desire, and excited because he was so incredibly close.

He growled, sounding more animal than man, and then attacked my lips with a vigor that literally electrocuted everything that lived beneath my skin.

He kissed me with a passion I never knew existed. With a possession that almost scared me. The way his lips moved over mine—demanding and rough—promised he would own me when all was said and done.

The hand cradling the back of my head flexed, digging in but not hurting. Delicious pressure erupted inside me. It started in my center and grew, making me moan and reach for him. My chin fell back as his lips drifted down my neck and scraped across my shoulder, which was bare because my dress slid down, exposing my skin.

I tried to get my hands beneath his shirt, but because of the way we were sitting, I couldn't find the hem. Instead, the back of my hand brushed across the undeniable hardness between his legs. The accidental contact made his entire body jerk and go rigid as a groan ripped from his mouth.

"Fuck, Katie."

"I-I'm sorry," I said, my voice low and shaky.

He pulled back, staring down at me with passion in his eyes. "Do it again."

My eyes widened, and even as my mouth worked to tell him it wasn't a good idea, my hand moved to do his bidding. This time, instead of the back of my hand, I used the pads of my fingers, brushing down the hard length in one single stroke.

His eyes fluttered closed and breath hissed between his teeth. A shudder moved through his body and in response, his member jerked toward me.

It was an intimidating size and my body stiffened.

Holt drew in a deep breath and then opened his eyes. Surprisingly, he sat me away from him, back onto my stool. He wiped a hand down his face and swore. "You're going to kill me."

Did that require a response?

An apology? A denial?

Before I could decide the appropriate way to address that statement, he pushed away from the counter and strode down the hallway, disappearing from sight.

It was kind of a relief.

Maybe now I could calm my racing heart.

10

Sexual tension. I never gave much thought to the term. I wasn't the kind of girl to sit around watching romantic comedies. I didn't read romance novels and I steered clear of Valentine's Day and everything associated with it. I didn't date and I stayed out of bars and other places where a man might think I was available. So sexual tension wasn't something I was familiar with. It wasn't something I ever thought I would experience.

Until now.

Four days of living with Holt and I was nothing but an exposed nerve, ready to explode at any moment. It was very confusing. It was very frustrating, and it was also kind of scary.

Yes, I'd been around men before. I'd lived with them. In fact, it was my experiences with the opposite sex that confirmed my decision to stay single. Forever. I was going to be one of those crazy ladies with fifty cats, a recliner, and a coupon addiction.

Except my cats were going to be books. Books were way less stinky than cats.

But now things were changing.

My world, my view, my feelings were starting to tilt, and it left me feeling a little unbalanced all the time.

I found myself wandering down the romance section of the library, perusing the plethora of covers with shirtless muscle-bound men. All the females were gorgeous, with long legs and looks of desire on their faces. I used to snort at the sight of these books and secretly snicker when I checked them out to the little old ladies that came here for a weekly book club meeting.

But now as I fingered the glossy covers, I wondered what was within the pages. I wondered what kind of role these buff, half-naked men played in the story. Were the heroines of the story just as affected by their leading men as I was by Holt?

Did they lie in bed at night with him just walls away and wonder what it would be like to lie with him in the dark while he touched every inch of skin he could find? Did they breathe in deep every time he stepped near just to get a whiff of the scent that only he carried? Did an accidental touch, the simple brush of a hand or a shared look that lingered too long, threaten to drive them insane?

I cleared my throat and put the book back on the shelf. Clearly, I had enough romance swirling around in my head without reading some book.

He hadn't kissed me since that first morning.

It seemed he went out of his way to give me some space, to keep a respectable distance between us. He wasn't distant and cold. He was friendly and open. Every night since I'd been there, we cooked dinner together, laughing and joking in the kitchen while I showed him how not to ruin a pan.

We played cards (I was terrible) and he let me win (because he was a sweet). We watched action movies and made up our own dialogue when we thought what the actors said was stupid. I did his laundry and he washed the dishes, and I continued to sleep in his bed while he remained on the couch.

If I didn't feel the attraction between us, if I didn't feel the way it lingered in the air around us, I would have thought he didn't see me as anything but a temporary roommate.

But I did feel it.

And he did too.

I could tell by the way his voice sometimes turned raspy and by the way he would watch me when he didn't think I saw. The way he would angle his body so he never had his back to me, so he was always somewhat open to my presence. And sometimes, when I laughed or when I ate, he would watch my mouth and a hungry glint would come into his eyes.

But if I hadn't noticed any of those things, I still would have known.

Every single night when I told him goodnight and he would whisper, "Sweet dreams," I would feel his stare on me until I turned the corner into his bedroom and climbed into his bed.

It was driving me mad.

For a girl who never thought about sex, who never desired that kind of relationship with a man... I sure was making up for lost time.

I knew it was better this way, that I couldn't act upon my feelings. This was only temporary—soon I would be going back to my life and he would go back to his. There was no use in complicating something that could remain simple.

With a sigh, I pushed all thoughts of Holt out of my head, glancing up at the clock. It was almost six. Closing time. I was tired today. It had taken two days of consistent work to get caught up here at the library. Things had really piled up while I was gone, but I finally managed to finish everything that needed to be done. All I had left was one cartful of books to put away, and then I could lock up for the night.

The last patron had left about an hour before, so I was alone in the building. Normally, I liked this time of the day, the peacefulness of being in a quiet place surrounded by books—of the passions of other people's minds. I enjoyed being able to be alone with my thoughts, but tonight felt different somehow.

The silence seemed ominous.

The peacefulness seemed disturbed by something unseen.

"It's just the rain," I murmured to myself, and as if on cue, the darkened sky lit up with lightning and thunder rumbled above the building. Southern thunderstorms were always a little creepy.

As I wandered down the aisles with my cart, replacing books to their designated place, I thought about what the police told me when Holt and I took them that letter.

Of course they were suspicious of Holt. They didn't understand why he wouldn't show them immediately.

Holt held firm, stating he wasn't about to discuss something that pertained to me until he had the chance to speak to me first. The police weren't as tickled by this as I secretly was, but eventually they moved beyond it and got to the matter at hand.

Even with an obvious threat against me, there still wasn't much to go on. The only thing they seemed clear on was that someone wanted to hurt me. They were, of course, going to be investigating. Taking prints off the letter (they didn't expect there to be any), looking for clues as to who could have sent it. They were questioning people at the WFD where Holt worked to see if anyone saw a person leave this note on Holt's windshield.

So far nothing.

And there had been no more fiery attempts on my life.

I didn't know what to think. Had the person given up? Was I safe? Or was the killer merely waiting for an opportunity to strike?

Like when you're alone in an empty library.

The thought caused me to look over my shoulder. Of course, no one was there, and I laughed lightly at my paranoia. Still, my footsteps quickened as I moved deeper into the shelves of books to finish my task.

A few minutes later, I heard the front door open and close. *Great,* I thought. *Only on nights when I am tired and ready to go home do people come in minutes before I lock up and expect me to stay late.*

The little bell on the front desk chimed and rolled my eyes. "I'll be right there," I called out, abandoning the cart and stepping down the aisle.

The bell started ringing again. Impatiently this time. *Ring, ring, ring, ring, ring!*

Irritation slammed through me. I knew they could hear me. It was so quiet in here, they would have to be deaf not to. Guilt followed the thought. Perhaps it was someone with a hearing problem.

I heard an odd scraping sound, a sound that caused me to pause and listen. It sounded as if someone were dragging something across the tiles that surrounded the front entrance and information desk.

Apprehension crawled up my legs like a long-legged spider, and my skin broke out in a cold sweat. I picked up the thickest, heaviest book nearby and held it out in front of me like a club, and I tentatively moved toward the sound.

I might be scared. But I wasn't going to run.

The sound of a scraping match echoed through the entire building and caused momentary spots to form before my eyes, blocking my vision. I sagged against a shelf and gave myself a mental pep talk. If it really was what I thought it was, I didn't have time to stand here and be scared. I had to act fast; I had to get out of the building.

Holding my breath, I turned the final shelf, stepping out into the open, facing the door and front entrance.

And that's when I saw it.

A cry ripped from my throat as I rushed forward.

The large metal trashcan that I kept behind the tall circular-shaped wooden information desk was now in front of the double glass doors.

And it was bursting with flames.

I have no idea how the flames got so high, so fast, but they were growing by the second. If I didn't do something, this entire building would go up like a bone-dry forest in California. All the books would be toast in minutes.

I tried not to shriek when I realized the flames were taller than me, and I cringed as the metal can began to distort and twist from the too-intense heat. I rushed past it, over to the wall where the fire extinguisher hung, and reached out to grab it.

But it was gone.

That meant two things:

One, I had to find another one and fast.

And, two, whoever started this fire was still in the building.

As much as I wanted to let fear and paranoia overtake me, I knew I couldn't. I had to put out this fire. And so I did something I always yelled at the TV for when dumb, big-chested idiots ran up the stairs when a killer was after them.

I ran toward the back of the library.

I knew where the other extinguisher was. It was the closest and I felt I could get it the fastest. I lugged the book as I ran, not willing to let go of my impromptu weapon just yet.

When the extinguisher came into view, I cried out in relief, thankful it was still there. With just a few feet between me and the red can, I lurched forward to grab it, and at the same time a very tall, very heavy shelf of books began to tip…

Everything that came next happened in excruciating slow motion.

I screamed, holding the giant book up above my head as if it would protect me, and turned back, trying

to jump out of the way of the falling shelf. Books of
all shapes and sizes began tumbling off the shelves,
raining paper and hardbacks. I deflected them as best
I could, lunging away and using the book like a
baseball bat to fend off the biggest that fell.

And then I tripped.

The bookshelf plunged after me.

11

I lurched forward, pitching myself to the side, and as I hit the ground, so did the shelf. It landed mere centimeters from my head.

Books piled on top of me, half covering my body. The silence that followed the crash was the quietest sound I ever heard.

Seconds ticked by and I began to move, to test my arms and legs, to take stock of my body and see if I was injured. I didn't think I was. My wrapped wrists were screaming in agony and I looked up, noting that one of the bandages was torn and my seared flesh was exposed.

I knocked away the books that covered me, pushing up to my hands and knees.

A pair of shoes stepped into my vision.

They appeared to be brand new, or at least rarely worn. They were a common brand, a man's shoe, but the feet were not nearly as large as the man's feet I'd become accustomed to seeing.

I lifted my head to look up, to see the face of the man trying to kill me, but before I could see anything, he kicked me.

The toe of his sneaker slammed into my already aching wrist. It buckled instantly, and I fell onto the ground with a sharp cry.

I cradled the injury to my chest as I rolled, nausea grabbing hold of my body and taking me for a spin. I shut my eyes tight, trying to swallow back the worst of the pain.

Get up!

Run!

Fight!

My brain demanded so much more than I wanted to give, but I knew I couldn't just lie here and let him kill me. And there was still the fire…

The man lifted his foot again and I prepared to fend off another blow, but then a shout from the front of the room caused us both to lose focus.

"Katie!" Holt roared. Just the sound of his voice made my body sing with joy.

"Back here!" I screamed as I rolled, picking up the giant book and throwing it at my stalker. He made a grunting sound as I jumped to my feet, and I turned to stare him in the face.

But he was running away with an oversized black hoodie over his head as he retreated.

"Stop!" I demanded, and to my own surprise I ran after him. He pushed through the emergency exit door and disappeared into a torrent of rain.

"Katie," Holt said, his voice much closer than before. I turned and saw him standing amongst the books and shelf, staring at me with gut-wrenching worry etched into the planes of his face.

"The extinguisher!" I cried, pointing. "The fire!"

He nodded swiftly, ripped the can off the wall, and then rushed out front. I ran after him, stopping to watch him release the white foamy spray. To my intense relief, the fire went out.

The double glass doors were covered in heavy black soot, but otherwise, nothing seemed to be too damaged except for the floor where the trashcan was sitting.

"What the hell happened?" he said, swinging around to face me.

My body was trembling all over from the rush of adrenaline and fear. My teeth were chattering and my body was shaking uncontrollably.

He was in front of me in two big steps and he opened his arms, pulling me against him and cradling me close. His hand rubbed vigorously up and down my arm as I pressed my face into his chest. With his free hand, he dialed his cell phone, speaking to someone and giving them information.

My ears didn't seem to be working. A weird kind of silence invaded my system, the kind of silence I didn't want. I pulled back, looking up at Holt. His lips moved, he was speaking, but I couldn't hear anything he was saying.

My vision began to dim and grow fuzzy.

Holt snapped his fingers directly in front of my face.

My knees began to buckle. He swept me up and walked toward the door, kicking it, and it buckled under his foot and swung open. He strode outside just as my vision went completely dark…

Icy pinpricks began to needle my skin. In seconds, I was completely drenched in water and a loud clap of thunder shook the sky above our heads.

A particular mean drop of rain landed against my tender flesh, the flesh that should have been covered.

I sprang awake. "Argh!" I yelled, tucking my wrists against Holt's chest.

He looked down at me, his short hair plastered to his head as water dripped off his nose and chin. "Stay with me, Freckles."

I nodded. "I'm okay now."

He eyed me skeptically.

"What is it with you and water? First the pool and now the rain," I cracked, trying to prove to him that I really was okay.

"Works, doesn't it?" He grinned and I couldn't help but notice how the rainwater outlined his full lips.

Yep, I was okay.

"Can we go back inside now?" I asked, hating the way my clothes clung to my skin.

"I don't know. I kind of like the view," he quipped, staring suggestively at my chest.

My shirt was white.

I was soaked.

My nipples were hard.

Any questions?

Surprisingly, I didn't move to cover myself. I let him look. Geez, in another couple months I'd be reading erotica if this kept up.

When I didn't protest to his stare, his eyes flashed to my face and then he turned around and went back inside. "Cops will be here in a few."

"I should probably call the branch manager."

Instead of standing me on the floor, he sat me down on top of the wooden desk and faced me. For once, I was eye level with him.

Without thinking, I reached out and brushed away a drop of water that was about to escape his eyebrow and drip into his eye.

His eyes darkened at my touch.

That electricity I was thinking about earlier flared between us. Thank goodness it wasn't a light because it would have blinded us both.

"Tell me what happened."

"He was here," I said, hoarse. "He lit the can on fire and took the extinguisher nearby. I ran to the back to get the other and he pushed one of the shelves over on me."

The muscles in Holt's jaw clenched and flexed beneath the stubble that lined his face.

"Do you ever shave?" I wondered out loud.

He smiled and rubbed at the gruffness. "I just trim it."

I nodded.

"Do you like it?" he asked.

Once again, I touched him, brazenly running my hand along his jaw. It was soft and rough at the same time—the perfect balance. "Yeah, I do."

"Good to know," he said, taking my hand, linking our fingers together, and then his face grew serious again.

"Obviously, I avoided the shelf."

"Did you get a look at his face?" I cringed at the hopefulness in his voice.

"No," I admitted. "I tried, but he kicked me."

His eyes went murderous. Maybe I shouldn't have said that.

"He. Kicked. You," he ground out, making each word into a pointed sentence.

This time I kept my mouth shut.

"Where?" he demanded.

I wasn't going to reply, but his eyes narrowed and I knew he would eventually make me tell him. I was going to have to tell the cops anyway. Weariness floated over me at the thought of enduring yet another one of their hours-long interrogations.

I lifted my wrist, the bandage just dangling from the area now, not covering or protecting a thing.

The waves of hatred that rolled off him made me sincerely glad that all that emotion wasn't directed at me. He stared at my delicately injured skin (some of it had gotten torn in the struggle and was slick with some sort of puss... Eww, gross), and I kind of thought the top of his head might explode.

I was going to reassure him that I was okay, but the police rushed inside, followed closely behind by a medic with a first aid kit.

"She needs medical attention," Holt barked, authority ringing through his tone. The medic hurried to comply, slamming down his kit and springing it open. Holt dropped his hand onto the man's shoulder and squeezed. "Bryant, I don't even want to see a flick of pain cross her face when you touch her."

Bryant looked at me and swallowed thickly. "Yes, Chief."

"*Chief?*" I said, looking up at Holt.

"I'll be right back," he said to me in a much gentler tone and then moved away.

Bryant was fumbling with his supplies, Holt's words clearly making him nervous. "Relax." I tried to soothe him. "He's just on edge about what happened.

[113]

I'm fine. I promise to smile the whole time you fix me up."

"But it's going to hurt," he blurted apologetically.

"Yeah, I know. Just do it. I'll be fine."

That seemed to calm him a little, and he got to work. It did hurt. Incredibly. I felt Holt's stare and I glanced up, giving him a fake smile. He rolled his eyes and turned back to one of the officers.

"Hey," I said to the medic. "Why did you call him chief?"

He gave me a quizzical look. "Arkain's the Wilmington Fire Chief."

My eyes jerked back to Holt where he stood talking to the police force and the firefighters that responded to the call. *His* firefighters. "I didn't realize," I murmured.

Bryant nodded. "I guess I can understand that. He's a humble guy. Doesn't like to throw his position around."

I made a sound of agreement as he applied something to my wrist that made my entire body jerk. I bit down on my lip to keep from crying out.

"I'm sorry!" he said a little too loudly. Holt stiffened and he turned, looking at me over his shoulder.

I blinked back the tears that flooded my eyes and waved at him with my free hand.

He said a few more words to the men standing around him and then he left them, coming to stand over poor Bryant.

I never realized how intimidating he was when he wanted to be.

"As soon as you're done, we're going home."

"But the police will want to talk to me," I protested.

"Not tonight. You've been through enough. They're going to come by the house tomorrow morning."

"You're acting very bossy right now," I warned, not really caring to be bossed.

"So are you saying you want to stay here and answer questions?"

"No."

He looked smug.

"I need to call the library director," I said, ignoring it.

He handed over his cell phone and watched as I dialed the number.

"So," Bryant said carefully, "you two live together?"

"No," I said at the exact same time Holt said, "Yes."

Well, this was awkward.

The director answered and saved me from more of the conversation. After that, I completely ignored Holt, Bryant, and the pain as I explained to my boss exactly what happened all the while hoping I still had a job.

12

I still had a job. However, I was put on a leave of absence so the library and its patrons would not be "subjected" to my stalker's murderous tendencies any longer. It was a paid leave of absence, thank goodness, because I truly needed the money and didn't relish trying to find another job and telling any potential employers that I may or may not be bait for trouble.

Most people might be happy about a forced paid vacation.

I wasn't one of them.

It left me feeling more like a kite merely drifting wherever the wind blew. Right now, in my eyes, I not only lost my home, all my material possessions, but my job as well. My entire life had blown up in my face. There was barely anything I recognized about myself anymore.

Here I was, living with a man I barely knew and wracked with all these feelings I didn't really understand. Everything I seemed to work toward for so long was snatched away and there was no safety net beneath me. I was freefalling through life, and it scared the living crap out of me.

What was I going to do all day now that I didn't have work to fill my time?

It was times like this a girl like me could use her mother. Someone to talk to who loved me unconditionally, someone who never judged me, someone who was merely there all the time—a never-ending constant.

But my mother wasn't here.

She never would be again.

I would have to get through this on my own.

And I would. Because I was tough.

By the time Holt pulled his truck into the driveway, the sun had set. We were at the library a lot longer than he wanted to be, but we ended up having to wait for my manager to get there so I could explain to her exactly what was going on. And after that, we stayed to reshelf the books and help clean up some of the mess.

Not that I was very helpful. I was literally exhausted and the pain in my wrists was terrible. I wanted nothing more than a shower and a bed. Holt finally dragged me out of there, ignoring my protests and stuffing me in the truck. Silently, I was glad he did.

When he turned off the engine, he didn't climb out. He leaned forward, using the steering wheel as a prop, and looked at me through the shadows inside the cab. "You're a lot stronger than you look."

I felt my lips curve. "Is that supposed to be a compliment?"

"You know it is. You've been handling everything better than most of the men I know would."

"Why didn't you tell me you were the fire chief?"

"Does it matter?"

"No." And it truly didn't. His job didn't make him who he was. I had no doubt the reason Holt had that job was *because* of who he was.

He climbed out of the truck then, coming around to my side and yanking open the door. I moved to get out, but he reached in and lifted me down, his touch once more so achingly gentle.

"All I'm saying," he said softly, "is if you need to cry, I have shoulder."

His words were exactly what I needed to hear. It made me feel like I wasn't as alone as I thought. "You're a good man, Holt Arkain." I reached up and touched his cheek. He grasped my hand and pulled it down to his mouth, pressing a few feather-light kisses to the inside of my palm.

It made me feel like all the strings that held me together inside had been untied and now everything was languid and free flowing.

"Come on," he whispered, keeping hold of my hand and leading me to the front door.

Once inside, I slipped off my flip-flops and just stared off into space. I was so tired and emotional. I just wanted to be alone. I heard the door lock behind us and it seemed to be the sign my body was waiting for—the sign that told my brain it was okay to fall apart.

"I'm really tired. I think I'm just going to go to bed."

I didn't wait for him to protest, which I knew he probably would. Instead, I just went quietly back to his room and closed the door. I didn't bother with the light. I liked the dark just fine. I didn't even bother taking off my top and skirt. I just climbed up into the bed and sank down in the center, grabbing a pillow and hugging it tight.

Then I buried my face in another pillow and began to cry.

I hated to cry. But in that moment, it seemed if I didn't release some of the things going on inside me, I might stop functioning.

I cried harder than I had in a very long time—only stopping when I had to let my face out of the pillow to suck in some much-needed air. Only the tears wouldn't stop, so I would end up burying my face all over again and repeating the process.

I don't know how long I lay there, but eventually I heard the door open. My entire body stiffened and my grip on the pillow increased to the point I thought the feathers filling it might come out the seam.

He didn't say anything as he crawled onto the bed behind me. His hand slid over my hip and he gently pulled me around so I was lying on my back and he was staring down at me through the darkness. "I can't stand to hear you cry anymore."

He heard? Damn, I was trying to be quiet.

"Come here," he murmured, settling down beside me, and pulled me alongside him. I fit up against him perfectly. He was so much bigger that he completely dwarfed me, and when I settled my head on his chest and he wound his arms around me, it was like I was completely surrounded by him. Like I was finally where I belonged. After all these years of searching, I finally found my place.

A few more tears leaked out and dripped on his shirt, but he didn't complain. "It's okay, Katie," he murmured, stroking my hair. "Everything's going to be okay."

"My entire life…" I said, pausing to drag in some air, "is a complete disaster."

"You have me."

For some reason those three words made me cry harder. Like the kind of cry that shook your insides and made ugly sounds rip from your throat. So very unattractive.

He didn't say anything. He held me, just like that night in the parking lot. He was a complete rock while chaos reigned around him.

When I was done with my ugly cry, I used his shirt to wipe my eyes. He chuckled. "Feel free to use my shirt as a tissue," he said dryly.

"Oh," I said, not even realizing what I'd done. "I—"

He tucked a strand of hair behind my ear. "Do you feel better?"

His tenderness was just more than I could bear. I started crying again. "I haven't washed my hair in a week," I sobbed, picking up his shirt and using it once again.

"You haven't?" he said, trying to hide the amusement in his voice.

"No. It hurts my hands and wrists too much." I dropped his shirt. "I smell!" I wailed.

That seemed to open the floodgates once again, and I swore if I didn't stop crying soon I was going to drown us both.

I guess Holt finally had enough because he extracted himself from my snotty clutches and got off the bed. When I thought he would leave, he turned back and picked me up off the bed. He walked into the bathroom across the hall (I refused to use his master bathroom, saying it was for him) and reached around the curtain to turn on the shower.

"What are you doing?" I asked suspiciously.

"Washing your hair."

"What? No, you can't!"

Visions of me having to get naked before him swam through my head and created a flurry of panic within me. Before I could wiggle out of his embrace, he was stepping in the shower—both of us fully clothed—and pulling the curtain closed behind us.

I shrieked when the water soaked my legs and feet. "Holt!" I gasped.

"Hold your arms out of the way," he instructed.

I did, pushing my arms up over my head so the fresh bandages wouldn't get ruined.

Then he stepped beneath the spray, drenching us both. "We're wearing clothes!"

"Do you want to get naked?" he drawled.

"I'm a virgin," I blurted out, and immediately I wanted to die of embarrassment.

Every muscle in his body stilled. I wasn't even sure he breathed.

Finally, after a few long, tense minutes, he looked at me. "Did I hear you right?"

I nodded miserably. What in the hell possessed me to say such a thing? It was the truth, but geez, talk about diarrhea of the mouth.

He stepped back out of the spray and set me down on my feet, my back facing the water.

I expected him to leave.

I didn't expect him to stay.

I didn't expect the words that came out of his mouth.

Carefully, he took my arms, looping them around his neck so my hands and wrists were behind his head, and then he took my face in his hands, lifting it up so he could stare down into my eyes.

"That makes me really happy, Freckles."

I blinked. "It does?"

He nodded slowly.

"The thought of anyone else's hands on you drives me insane. Now I get to be your first. And your last."

Oh my.

He lowered his head, pressing a very brief kiss to my lips before pulling away and using his hands to tilt my head back. Warm water poured over my scalp, saturating my hair and making me moan.

"You're really gonna wash my hair?" I asked.

"I don't get into showers fully clothed for any other reason," he drawled.

"We look ridiculous."

"Who cares?"

I surrendered then. To his touch. To the feel of his hands in my hair. He used a lot of shampoo, so he spent an absurd amount of time massaging it in and running it through the thick mass of my water-logged strands. Then he rinsed it all out, the suds clinging to our clothes and bubbles floating around us in the tiny enclosed space.

He even conditioned it, taking care to work the stuff through the ends of the tangled mess.

"That feels so good," I murmured. I don't think I'd ever felt anything so pleasant in my entire life. It was as if the whole world fell away; all my responsibilities and all my stress just seemed to slip right down the drain with the suds he rinsed away.

As he worked, I was treated to the close-up view of his soaked shirt plastered to his chest. It molded perfectly against his ripped chest and abs. I could see every muscle, every plane of his body. I wondered how often he had to work out to look that way.

Suddenly I was self-conscious about what I looked like. I knew my shirt was see-through. I knew it was likely plastered to me the same way his was, except I didn't look like that. I was thin, with not so many curves and small breasts. He was all tan, smooth, and tall with rippling muscles. I was small, freckled, and pale with no muscle definition at all.

"Watch your wrists," he said, stepping back.

I held them up and out, thinking he was going to go get us some towels.

He took off his shirt.

I must have gaped because he paused. "Is this okay?"

I could only stare at the way the droplets of water clung to his skin and slid down… down into the waistband of his low-slung jeans.

"I just wanted to use it," he said softly, stepping toward me cautiously like I was a bird with a broken wing. "To do this." He used the end of the shirt to wipe my face and eyes, cleaning away what was left of my tears and what happened earlier.

I started to close my eyes again, but I forced them to remain open. I wanted the satisfaction of seeing him, of getting an eyeful of all that skin.

My arms began to feel tired from holding them out for so long, but I ignored the burning and continued to look my fill. His chest was completely hairless and it glistened beneath the water.

I found myself reaching out toward him, just wanting to see what he would feel like.

He shook his head slowly. "You'll get wet."

"I don't care."

He smiled. "I do. Bryant did a good job on those bandages. You need to leave them on all night."

I sighed, robbed of something I wanted so badly. He gave a deep chuckle and directed both my arms back around his neck to rest on his shoulders.

"Can I touch you, Katie?" he asked, his voice husky and low.

I nodded, wanting more of the way he made me feel before.

He started at my elbow, running his hand down toward my armpit where he skimmed lightly over the sensitive skin and continued down my side, leaving a trail of heat wherever he went. I was wearing a white top that buttoned up the front. It was an A-line style, so it was tighter up top and then sort of floated out around my waist. The skirt I wore was snug and black; it fell at a modest length (because it was for work) but still above the knee. I'd been careful about the choices I made when I picked up some new clothes. I needed pieces I could wear for work and more casually because I was only able to buy a few things.

It was a cute outfit, but right now I hated it. It felt like a block of concrete covering my skin. It was a too-thick barrier between him and me.

His hands went to the buttons, fingering them, playing with them. "We don't have to do anything you don't want to do. I'm not trying to push you, or rush you."

I swallowed thickly as he pulled at one of the buttons, gauging my reaction. I wanted to scream for him to rip it off already, but I didn't.

When I didn't say anything, he bent so he was looking directly into my eyes. "I just want to explore you. I want to really see you. We'll leave our bottoms on, okay?"

"It's no fair," I said.

He looked at me with a quizzical look in his eyes and tilted his head to the side.

"You get to touch me, but I can't touch you."

His smile was slow and sly. "Good. I don't want to share this moment. Not even with you. I'm going to be purely selfish right now, Katie. I've been longing to touch you like this since that first night you stayed here. This is my turn. Your turn can wait."

He said nothing else as he slowly began to unbutton my top. Even after it was completely open, it didn't fall away like it would have if I were dry. It clung to my body, still concealing most of my skin.

He used his index finger to slowly trace a line, starting at the waistband of my skirt and slipping upward, right in the center of my stomach and chest where my shirt was slightly parted.

I shivered at the way it felt.

When he got to the top, he used both his hands to slip beneath the edges and push it down, only it wouldn't go very far because my arms were up. I gave a nervous giggle and lowered them, still keeping them out of the spray of the shower. He peeled off the shirt, taking extra care to watch my injuries. He moved so slow that I became impatient and made a sound in the back of my throat.

He tossed the shirt over the shower curtain as the warm spray slid over my shoulders.

Thank goodness I bought a pretty bra.

All my bras I had before were no-nonsense, plain things that served their purpose. But when I went shopping the other day, I gravitated toward the lacy, girly undergarments for reasons I didn't understand.

But now I did.

My subconscious was secretly hoping that someone (Holt) would see them.

It was a peach tone, made almost completely of lace with a little tiny bow in the center. The straps were silky and smooth, and when I put it on, I instantly fell in love with it.

I glanced up at his face, wondering if he liked it too. I noticed his hands kind of floated over my body, not quite touching but too close to call it anything but. He was looking at me with a sort of awe in his eyes that made me feel silly for ever thinking I wouldn't be anything but beautiful in his eyes.

A quick glance down told me what I already knew. Wet, the bra was practically see- through. He wouldn't need to take it off because it left nothing to the imagination.

He fingered the straps, watching me, and when I made no sound of refusal, his touch became a little bit bolder. He cupped my breasts in his hands, gently massaging them, and edging his fingers just inside the top of the cups.

My breath caught at the unexpected sensations that fired through me. Without thought, my back arched, pushing myself farther into his palms. His thumbs traced a circle around my nipples, then flicked over the hardness, causing my thighs to squeeze together. His playing with my chest was causing an ache in my panties.

Next, his hands splayed my waist, holding me firmly as he dipped his head and began to kiss my chest. His mouth was hot and the water was beginning to turn cool. But I didn't care. I would stand there under the iciest of water as long as he didn't stop.

He suckled on my skin, something I didn't know anyone would want to do, as he slowly made his way lower until he sucked my breast right into his hot mouth.

He used his tongue to massage the nipple, and a groan ripped from my throat.

My hands moved to his head, wanting to hold him there, but he made a sound in his throat reminding me I wasn't supposed to touch him.

How was I expected to follow those rules when the things he was doing to me were driving me mad?

After he fully endowed attention on one breast, he moved over, bestowing the same exact treatment on the other. By this time, my legs were shaking, my skin was rippled with gooseflesh, and my panties were wet—and not from the water.

The sensations overcoming me were so powerful that I was a little embarrassed.

He lifted his head. "The water's cold."

I just nodded, my lips not able to form a response.

He reached around me and shut off the spray. Before pulling away, he dipped his head and kissed me. It was slow and gentle; he coaxed my tongue right out of my mouth and into his.

Then he was wrapping me in a towel and drying off my skin. He paid more attention to some parts than others, but I really didn't care.

"I'll be right back. I'll get us some dry clothes."

When he was gone, I sank down on the toilet, pressing a hand to my lips. I was falling for him. I was falling so hard and so fast that I didn't know how to stop it. I didn't think I could.

Was I ready for this? Would I be able to handle this along with everything else I was dealing with right now?

My head said no.

My heart whispered *yes*.

The bathroom door opened and he handed me in some clothes and then shut the door behind him. I hurried to strip away what was left on my body, taking a minute to drape the wet items over the curtain rod. Then I hurried to comb out my hair and grabbed up the clothes.

A pair of panties and one of his T-shirts. That's what he brought me.

I smiled the entire time I dressed.

Thankfully, the bandages around my wrists appeared to be in good shape, barely wet, and I was glad I wasn't going to have to bother with them tonight. I was feeling too blissful to deal with the pain.

When I stepped out of the bathroom, he was there leaning against the wall, waiting. He was dry and dressed in a pair of basketball shorts and no shirt.

I would never get tired of seeing him without a shirt.

He pushed away from the wall, his eyes sweeping over me in his shirt, and I knew by the look in his eyes he liked what he saw.

My entire life I've never been concerned with pleasing others, but I desperately wanted to please him.

"You're beautiful," he told me.

"I think you are, too."

"Goodnight, Freckles." He kissed me on the forehead, his lips lingering, and then he pulled away.

I caught his arm as he turned. "Holt?"

"Anything," was his reply.

Butterflies erupted in my belly. "Will you sleep with me?"

He glanced inside his room at the bed, then back at me. "Only if you promise not to try to take advantage of me." He widened his eyes like he was somehow scandalized.

I laughed. "Please. You'd like it."

"You're damn right."

I followed him into the bedroom. He pulled back the blankets and then gestured for me to get in. Once I was settled, he climbed in behind me, pulling the sheets up around us both.

My body still tingled from the shower, and I rolled to face him, leaning over to kiss him. Finally, my hand was free from the fear of water, and I was able to run it over his bicep and slip across his chest.

"Oh, no you don't," he murmured against my lips, placing a hand over mine to stop it in its tracks.

"You don't want me to touch you?"

"Oh, honey, do I ever. But not tonight. I'm a patient man, but I'm no saint. Your hot little body has already pushed me to my limit."

I frowned, thinking that might not be a good thing.

He must have read my silence because he laughed. I saw his teeth flash in the dark. "Tomorrow. You can have your turn tomorrow."

He pulled me down against his chest and sighed. I snuggled just a little bit closer.

Suddenly it felt like Christmas. I knew the sooner I went to sleep, the sooner tomorrow would be here.

The sooner I would be able to unwrap my present... or in this case, the sooner I'd be able to unwrap Holt Arkain.

13

The police came knocking at the crack of dawn
the next day. Okay, it was after nine, but we were still
in bed. Turns out he is really warm and really
comfortable and it makes waking up impossible.

But when the cops knock, you answer.

Unless, of course, you're a criminal. Then you
probably run out the back door.

But I wasn't a criminal and I wasn't running
anywhere.

Still, I wasn't happy about it. While Holt
answered the door, I stumbled around looking for a
pair of pants. I finally found some shorts and pulled
them on. I was reluctant to take off his shirt, but I
knew I couldn't leave it on. For one thing, it was so
long if I walked out there with it on, it would appear I
wasn't wearing pants.

That wouldn't be appropriate.

But I wondered what Holt's face would look
like...

It was almost enough to get to me try it out.

But at the last minute, I peeled it off and threw on a tank top with a built in bra. My wrists were still really sore from last night and all I could think about was a pain pill.

Okay, and Holt.

More specifically, today was supposed to be my day for touching.

It seemed a little alien to me that just yesterday I'd been a little nervous and feeling insecure, but today I was feeling more bold… more willing to give things a try.

I was smiling when I walked out into the living room. All eyes turned to me. Then I remembered I didn't comb my hair. I likely looked like I stuck my finger in a light socket.

I grimaced and wondered if they would think it was weird if I ran from the room in search of a brush.

I glanced at Holt. He wagged his eyebrows at me.

Clearly, he would be no help.

"If it's all right, Miss Parker, we would like to speak with you about the events that took place last evening at the library."

"Of course," I replied, giving up on my hair and going over to sit on the couch.

And so the questions began.

This time they were more involved, more detailed because I'd actually seen someone. It didn't matter that I didn't get a look at his face; they seemed to think I probably did and just didn't realize it because I was so scared. I begged to differ. I knew when I looked at a person's face and when I didn't.

However, they still wanted me to meet with a sketch artist to draw what I saw. I thought it was stupid, but I agreed to it anyway. I certainly wasn't going to do anything that might slow down the case. I wanted this person caught. I wanted my life back.

I wanted my life back—didn't I?

After I told them everything at least three times, they still said the same thing to me. "We're investigating. Be cautious." Then, they finally left.

The minute Holt shut the door behind them, I went into the kitchen and reached for my pain medicine and a bottle of water.

"How's the pain?" he asked, eyeing the way I clutched the bottle.

It sucked. "Better than last night."

He gave me a look that said he knew I was lying, but he didn't call me out.

After I took my medicine and downed half the water, I said, "There's a couple things I need to get at the store. I can pick up something to make for dinner while I'm out. If there's anything you need, let me know and I'll pick it up for you."

Staying here was hard to swallow sometimes because he wouldn't let me give him money for rent or utilities. I didn't like thinking I was mooching off him or he was taking care of me. I liked taking care of myself. The ability to take care of myself was very important to me because I was someone that would never let me down. I was someone who always looked out for me. I realized Holt was being far more supportive than most, but I still didn't want to lean too much on him because that would make standing up straight again that much harder.

Finally, I got him to agree to let me pay for the groceries. And then my time in the kitchen sort of became impromptu cooking lessons, so at least I felt I was repaying him even if it was in a small way.

"I have to work today," he said as he glanced at the clock.

"Are you late?" I wondered, thinking he usually went in early when he had to work.

"Yeah,"

My eyes widened. I made him late! I wallowed all over him in bed and caused him to miss his alarm.

He chuckled, taking in my expression. "Relax, I told them last night I would be late on account of the police coming by today. Their visit is technically work related."

Relief poured through me. "Do you have to spend the night tonight?"

Since I'd been here, he had yet to pull an overnight shift, but I knew it was something he often did. It was only a matter of time before he announced he wasn't coming home. The thought of him not being here tonight was very disappointing for two reasons:

One, I didn't relish the idea of being in his home alone.

And, two, if he wasn't here, I couldn't look at him without his shirt.

"Normally, yes," he began, and I hid my regret, but then he said, "But a couple of the guys agreed to take my night shifts so I could be here."

It made me wonder how much he told the guys he worked with about my situation. Surely they were curious after responding to three incidents involving me. I wondered what his relationship with them was like. Was it a formal "yes, sir" "no, sir," or was it more friendly and open?

"Oh, well, I hope it isn't taking them away from their families."

His eyes softened at my concern over his coworkers' lives. "It's not. I've taken a lot of the overnight and weekend shifts the past year since I was separated and divorced from Taylor. They owe me."

His mention of Taylor left me feeling a little sick. I didn't like to think of her perfect Barbie hands touching him.

I murmured some sort of agreement and then moved past him to go tame the nest of hair on my head before heading out.

"Where do you think you're going?" he said, catching me around the waist and towing me backward.

"To brush my hair?"

To my astonishment, he began to nuzzle the side of my neck. I felt his deep inhale of breath and thought, *Did he just smell me?*

Tingly shivers raced across my skin, all the way down to the floor where my toes curled against the linoleum. Brushing away my hair, his lips moved across my neck, pressing moist, gentle kisses to my extremely sensitive flesh. One of his arms wrapped around me from behind, pulling me fully up against his body. It certainly didn't escape my attention that there was something very hard and very large poking me in the back.

Apprehension slithered like an unwanted guest up my spine. I had no idea how something like that was supposed to fit into someone like me. My body certainly didn't seem to think it would be a problem, but my brain wasn't so sure.

I turned my head to the side and he moved up, capturing my lips in an all-encompassing kiss. Slowly, he spun me around so I faced him and he could fully claim my mouth. Before pulling his head away, he cupped my butt, giving it a gentle squeeze and then looking down at me with a thoroughly satisfied smile on his face. "Good morning."

Something had changed between us. Last night was the first time since our morning kiss in the kitchen. I'd thought after that kiss he wasn't interested because of the way he pulled away. But now… now we felt closer. The magnetic energy that pulsed between us was harder to ignore.

"What's the matter, Freckles?" he said, pressing a light kiss to the tip of my nose.

"What changed?" I blurted out.

He drew back. "Changed?"

"You seemed like you were trying to keep distance between us before, but after last night…"

"I should get a medal for managing to keep my hands off you that long."

"It was only a few days," I reminded him dryly.

"Felt like a lifetime."

"So those first kisses… you liked them?"

His eyes widened. "You thought that I didn't?"

"Well, after that you didn't touch me."

"Shit," he swore beneath his breath and ran a hand over his head. "I liked it *too* much. The sparks between us are so hot, I was afraid I wouldn't be able to stop. I was afraid I would scare you off. Thank God I did because you're so innocent."

Innocent? Ugh.

I folded my arms across my chest. "So what changed your mind?"

His smile was sexy and filled with innuendo. "I realized you could handle the heat."

I still wasn't so sure, but I didn't tell him that. "Well, you are definitely hot."

He grinned. He had such a big ego. "How hot?"

I shook my head. "So hot your touch leaves torch marks on my skin."

He whistled between his teeth. "Damn. I'm good."

I patted his chest. "I'm going to get ready."

I ended up just pulling my hair up into a topknot on my head, not even bothering to try to tame the frizz. It was one of the reasons I was going out. I needed some serum to help tame it. And I also needed some body lotion, some more disposable razors, and a few other girl necessities. If Holt was going to be touching me a lot more, then I needed to look good.

I shoved my feet in a pair of flip-flops and grabbed the canvas navy-blue purse I got off the clearance rack at Target, containing my library ID, a lip gloss, and new bank cards. Thankfully, the bank got new ones to me immediately to save me many trips to the bank itself.

I still didn't have a wallet or any of the other items I used to carry around, but it was better than nothing at all.

I made it all the way to the front door when I realized I was forgetting something essential.

I didn't have a car.

It was still being looked at for evidence.

Holt came out of the hallway a few minutes later, dressed for work in a pair of dark jeans and a white button-down shirt, sleeves rolled up around his elbows and collar open at the throat.

"What's the matter?"

Cambria Hebert

"I forgot I don't have my car."

"Well, that is a problem."

I shrugged. "I'll call a cab. While I'm out, I'll stop by and bug the police for my car."

"You're not taking a cab."

"Why not?"

"Because I have no idea who drives those things. They probably don't even have real driver's licenses."

I snorted. "Yeah, right. Isn't that illegal?"

"So is arson and murder," he said seriously.

I felt the color drain from my face.

"I'm not trying to scare you." He sighed.

He didn't really; I was already scared.

"You can take my truck."

My eyes about fell out of my head. "I thought no girls were allowed to drive your truck."

"You're not just any girl."

"I'm not?"

He shook his head.

I glanced out the window toward the driveway where his very huge, very shiny truck sat. "It's too big."

"No, it's not."

"I'll hit things."

His eyes narrowed. "You better not."

"I'll just stay here."

"You'll be bored in five minutes."

I'd rather be bored than driving that thing over curbs.

"Come on," he called, going out the front door. "You can drop me off at work."

I followed along behind him, hoping I wouldn't regret this.

14

Three telephone books. That's how many he had to pile on the seat so I could see over the dashboard.

I wasn't embarrassed.

Nope.

Mortified, uncomfortable, and vaguely amused just about covered how I felt while firefighters piled out of the station to watch their chief stack phone books into the driver's seat of his cherry-red pick-up and then hoist me up inside.

Never mind the fact I felt like I had to stretch my leg all the way out to press the gas pedal.

I giggled as I turned into the parking lot of Target (it's my favorite store) remembering the slightly greenish cast to Holt's skin as I drove away. When I raised my hand to wave to him, the green turned much deeper and he yelled, "Both hands on the wheel!"

I mean really, why did he insist I drive the truck at all?

It was a nice vehicle, but it was really big and I imagined driving it felt a lot like driving a boat. It seemed to bounce over the road, dipping over every little bump or unevenness in the pavement.

I parked about a mile away from the entrance. I was terrified of sideswiping another car or getting it stuck in a spot I wouldn't be able to back out of. So I settled on the very last space in the lot and pulled through so I would be able to drive right out when I left.

I didn't really feel like shopping, but I didn't have anything better to do, so I wandered around for quite a while, looking at things I didn't need and looking at other things I wish I could afford. I wandered into the home section and caught myself picking out things that would look great in Holt's place. Throw pillows for the bed, art for the walls, kitchen utensils that could possibly withstand his attempts at a meal. When I realized what I was doing, I stood there looking around like someone caught me with my dress tucked into my pantyhose and toilet paper trailing from the bottom of my shoe. I hightailed it to the makeup section before I ended up at the jewelry counter staring at diamond rings.

Not going to happen, I reminded myself because clearly, I needed a reminder.

After that, I got down to business, selecting razors, tweezers, hair products, and all the other basics a girl might need. My eye strayed to some really beautiful hairclips, but I didn't bother to pick them up because they cost too much money.

Sighing, I turned away, catching movement out of the corner of my eye. I looked swiftly, only to see something dark disappear around the end of the aisle.

I couldn't help the way my heart rate picked up or the slight tremor in my hands.

It's just someone shopping. I reassured myself.

Even still, I headed away from the section, peering down the aisles as I passed. About three rows down, I saw him.

A man with a dark hoodie.

Everything in my cart toppled over with the force of my halting stop.

What the hell are you doing? my mind demanded. *Run!*

But it was too late. The person heard my fumble and turned, pushing back the hoodie and looking in my direction.

Long blond hair spilled out around her shoulders. She gave me a strange look as I stood there and gaped. I tried to smile and not sound like a complete stalker. "Sorry! I thought you were someone else." And then I moved away, silently cursing myself.

I grabbed a couple boxes of the power bars that I noticed Holt liked to eat and then wandered over toward the sleepwear. I gazed at all their cute pajamas, with the tank tops and matching bottoms. The nightgowns were feminine and pretty with bows and polka dots. I thought about getting something... something I could wear to bed in case Holt decided to sleep with me again tonight.

But in the end I didn't.

Because if I bought those pajamas, I wouldn't need his T-shirt.

I made my way to the checkout counter, feeling tiny pinpricks of warning on the back of my neck. I felt creepy... I felt watched.

I glanced around, but no one appeared to be staring.

Quickly, I paid for my items and piled the bags into the cart. I could have carried them all, but with my wrists still hurting and the mile I had to walk to the truck, I decided I would just use the cart.

Outside, the summer southern heat blasted me, and I paused to dig in one of the bags for the new pair of sunglasses I picked out. They were white with wide oval-shaped lenses. Once they were in my hand, I checked the street and then continued out, fumbling with the tag hanging from the frame of my shades.

I heard the acceleration of an engine but didn't look up.

Not until the screeching of tires seemed entirely too close and someone across the parking lot gave a shout.

My head snapped up.

Time slowed.

The car did not.

At the very last second, I swung the cart in front of me and dove to the side, slamming into a parked car and falling onto the hot asphalt.

The sound of crunching metal pierced my ears.

I was aware of the car squealing away, and then there were people surrounding me, trying to help me off the ground.

A man with jeans and a black T-shirt leaned over me. "Holy shit! Are you all right? He tried to run you down."

I looked up at him, pressing a hand to my forehead. Everything was tilted and dizzy.

"I'm calling the cops," he said and yanked out a cell phone. That's when I noticed his shoes. They were brand new or rarely worn. A common men's brand.

I lurched up from the pavement, reaching out a hand to steady myself against the car nearby. The man reached out to help me, and I jerked away before he could touch me.

"No need to call the police. I'm fine."

His eyes about fell out of his head. He was young, maybe my age. He didn't look like the type of guy that would try to burn me to death. More than once. I hated the fact that I was instantly suspicious of everyone around me.

Of course, what did I expect? For him to walk around wearing a T-shirt that said PYRO across the front?

Unlikely.

"Lady, that guy just tried to run you down!"

"Yeah, I was there," I snapped. I was really getting tired of someone trying to kill me.

"You need to call the cops," said a woman standing nearby.

"Did anyone get his plates? A description? Anything?" I asked. Anything at all would be helpful.

Everyone looked around blankly at each other.

The guy with the sneakers spoke up. "It was a man. He was wearing glasses and a dark hoodie."

My knee was scraped from where I fell and I could feel the warm blood oozing down my lower leg.

"Thank you," I told him, trying not to look at his shoes and scream. I knew he wasn't the one trying to kill me, but it drove me crazy that I felt like I couldn't trust anyone. How was I supposed to carry on with my life and not stare at every man wearing these shoes or a dark hoodie? Is this how my life was going to be from now on—me looking over my shoulder, searching every face for a sign they were the one?

Sneaker man watched me warily. I mustered what smile I could and said, "Thank you for offering me help. I really appreciate it."

"You really don't want me to call the cops?"

"No. There's nothing they can do. He's gone."

Someone else approached and I tensed, expecting some sort of attack. A young couple held out my bags, offering me my spilled purchases.

"I think we got everything," the girl said sympathetically. She had a long blond ponytail and really pretty skin.

I thanked them and then bent to pick up everything that dumped out of my purse when I fell.

The crowd started to thin, thankfully, and all I wanted to do was leave. Gripping the bags in both hands, I stepped away from the car on unsteady legs and looked at the truck, which stood like a beacon in the distance.

But then I remembered my sunglasses.

I must have dropped them in my haste to not become road kill.

They were lying in the street.

Beside the shopping cart.

It was completely dented and one of the wheels had fallen off.

I reached down and picked up the sunglasses. They were snapped in half and one of the lenses was shattered.

What a shame, I thought. *What a waste of good eyewear.*

Torch

A hysterical laugh bubbled up in my throat, and I swallowed it, trekking the distance to the truck, tossing my bags inside and then hoisting myself in.

Once there, I collapsed against the seat, trying to calm the shaking of my hands.

It could have been an accident.

I knew it wasn't.

15

I went home. I only hit a couple curbs along the way, one of them being in front of the house.

I let myself inside and proceeded to check every room and closet to make sure there were no murderers lurking, and then I went into the bathroom and cleaned up the scrape and drying blood on my leg.

Thank goodness he had a first aid kit beneath the sink because I needed a bandage.

After that I curled up on the couch, inhaling Holt's scent on the cushions. I flipped through the channels on TV, looking for something that might take my mind off the fact someone out there wanted me dead.

It wasn't something I could wrap my brain around easily. It seemed one minute I was shelving books, going treasure hunting at flea markets, and wondering what type of candy to eat when I watched a movie, and the next I was constantly chased by a burning flame, looking over my shoulder when I went out in public, and living with a man I just met.

Mom always said the key to life was playing the cards you were dealt. Well, how could I play when I didn't understand the game?

A commercial for some entertainment "news" show that came on at night broke into my thoughts, causing me to look up.

New details on last month's death of iconic rocker Tony Diesel have been released. The autopsy report confirms that his sudden and shocking death was caused by an accidental drug overdose. Tony was buried weeks ago in an exclusive Beverly Hills cemetery. The service was not open to the public. Now that the cause of death is confirmed, all attention will be directed…

I picked up the remote and changed the channel, completely uninterested in celebrity gossip.

I didn't know who Tony Diesel was. I didn't listen to rock music. I thought it sounded like a bunch of men screaming unintelligible words into a microphone. I preferred pop and country music. But it did seem like he and I had something in common.

Neither one of us was too good for death.

It didn't matter how much money you had, how famous you were, or how badly you just wanted to be left alone. A drug overdose seemed like a pretty crappy way to die. Of course I really didn't know of any good ways to die.

I shook my head. I was being weird and morbid. All these thoughts about death and dying. Checking the closets and the showers for lurking killers. This wasn't reality. This was a nightmare, and I badly wanted to wake up.

And since I was already awake, that didn't really seem like an option.

So I decided to be in denial.

I was going to sit here and watch an infomercial on hair loss for men and pretend I didn't have a care in the world.

Okay, I wasn't going to watch that. It was ridiculous.

I flipped around until I found a marathon of *The Vampire Diaries*.

At least the men on that show weren't balding.

I immersed myself in love triangles and teen drama for the rest of the day. It was actually pretty entertaining. Even still, when it was time to pick up Holt, I was glad. I'd missed him all day. And it wasn't because I'd been scared. There had been a lot of times in my life when I was scared or unsure, and I never missed anyone; I only ever counted on myself.

I missed Holt because... well, *because*.

I wasn't going to think about that either.

As I was walked out to the truck (I parked it on the road so I wouldn't have to back out of the driveway) a car was driving down the street. Normally, I wouldn't have thought anything of it, except for the fact someone had just tried to mow me down.

Instead of moving toward the truck, I stopped in the center of the yard and stared at the car as it crept by. It wasn't a dark sedan like the car in the Target parking lot. It was a silver BMW.

I swear it slowed down as it passed the yard where I stood. The windows were so darkly tinted that I couldn't see who sat inside. I waited until the car turned off the street before bolting to the truck and shutting myself inside.

At the end of the street, I stopped, making sure no one was behind me, and put the truck in park to adjust the phone books beneath my butt. One was sliding loose and it was very uncomfortable.

Once that was finished, I put the truck back in drive and glanced down the street before pulling out. The silver BMW was parked a few houses down at the curb.

Strange, I thought and pulled out. About four houses down in the opposite direction, the BMW pulled out onto the road and followed me.

Call me crazy, but this probably wasn't good.

My grip on the steering wheel tightened; my knuckles turned white. I told myself to calm down, that it was probably someone just driving to wherever they had to be. But that didn't stop me from compulsively checking the rearview mirror to see if they were still there every three seconds.

They were.

It was a man, if I wasn't mistaken. He had very short hair and sunglasses on his face. I couldn't make out anything more, and I needed to keep my attention on driving. I thought about calling Holt, but then I remembered I didn't get a new cell phone yet.

I came to a rather large intersection and figured this would be the place he would turn. He would go right toward the more congested area with the shops and restaurants, and I would go left toward the firehouse.

But that isn't how it happened.

I turned and so did he, getting bolder and moving right up behind me. He trailed so close behind that when I looked in the rearview, I couldn't see his front bumper. Nerves cramped my stomach and I fidgeted in my seat. Sweat slicked my palms, making the steering wheel slippery as I drove.

Almost there.

The man following along behind me laid on his horn. I jumped and one of the phone books slid off the stack. I sat up as high and straight as I could and scooted to the edge of the seat, pressing down on the gas a little more. The large engine responded immediately and I shot forward.

The BMW shot forward as well.

When I looked in the rearview, I noted he wasn't only tailgating me and laying on his horn, but now he had his arm out the window, shaking it at me.

His arm was covered in dark fabric.

Panic took over.

The fire station came into view, and I put the pedal to the metal. The truck ripped up the street, the tires peeling against the road and kicking up a little smoke. I didn't care. I kept going, driving as fast as I could. I almost overshot the parking lot, but I slammed on the brakes, jerked the wheel, and drove up over the curb. I skidded to a stop in the center lane, not in a parking spot and not giving two shits.

I shoved open the door as one of the men came around a giant fire engine, confusion on his face. I jumped to the ground, stumbling a bit, my wrist taking some of the fall, and I cried out.

The BMW pulled into the lot behind me, the car screeching to a halt. The driver's door opened so the man could climb out.

"Help me!" I cried, pushing up and rushing toward the fireman. "That man is chasing me!"

I dashed forward and he caught me by the shoulders, his gaze sharpening on the other man behind me.

"He tried to run me off the road!"

Other men were spilling out of the garage now, assessing the situation and forming a circle around me.

"Katie," the man yelled, and I turned, looking around at the guys surrounding me. My pursuer was an older man with broad shoulders and a tan.

"Oh my God, he knows my name," I told the man still gripping my shoulders. His dark eyes narrowed on my face and his mouth pulled into a grim line.

"He won't get near you," he promised.

The man rushed forward and I shrieked.

He was intercepted by several very angry firefighters. He tried to push through them, still intent on getting to me. I heard him speak but didn't hear his words.

And then one of the men drove his fist into the man's face and he crumpled to the ground.

My entire body slumped with relief.

The loud bang of a door swinging open and hitting a wall made me jump and look toward the firehouse. Heavy footsteps pounded inside the garage, drawing closer as Holt yelled my name.

When I caught a glimpse of him, my entire body gave a great sigh. The men around me parted, giving him a path directly to me. He stopped just shy of yanking me into his arms, his eyes sweeping over every inch of me before settling on my face.

"I didn't wreck your truck," I said, trying to sound anything other than completely terrified.

And then I was in his arms. My face buried against the strength of his chest.

Finally, I was safe.

16

"Shouldn't we have stayed?" I asked him, glancing out the rear window as we drove away from the fire station.

"If we stayed, I would have killed him."

"Oh. Well, I guess it's good we left, then."

"Do you want to explain to me why I want to kill that guy back there?"

I told him exactly what happened, leaving out the part about almost getting run at Target. I figured it wouldn't help his murderous tendencies.

Look at me, joking about murder. It really just wasn't funny.

"He knew my name," I whispered. I think that was the part that bothered me the most.

Holt held out his arm and I slid across the seat and fit myself into his side. A few minutes later, we arrived back at his house and that made me think of something else.

"He knows where we live." And that took something away from me that I didn't even realize I had. Security. The walls of this house made me feel protected, made me feel like I didn't have to be scared all the time.

"If anybody wants in that house, Katie, they're gonna have to go through me."

That didn't make me feel better. It made me feel worse. I didn't want any kind of harm to come to him while he tried to protect me.

Inside, I retreated to the bathroom to wipe my face with a cool rag and calm my tattered nerves. Holt was in the kitchen scrounging through the cupboards and that's when I realized I hadn't gone grocery shopping.

"I forgot to get something for dinner," I said from the edge of the room.

"Want to go out?"

"Sure." It would be better than sitting around here and waiting for something bad to happen. "I'm just going to shower really fast." I thought maybe it would help wash away some of the crazy I was involved in today.

Holt nodded and kept scrounging around for a snack. I remembered the power bars I bought and went to get them out of the sack I had dumped on the bed and ignored.

"Here," I said, handing over the two boxes. I was hoping he didn't notice how the boxes were mashed and mangled looking.

"What the hell happened to these?"

"I dropped them," I mumbled and turned to flee into the shower.

"What happened to your knee, Katie?" The edge in his voice stopped me in my tracks.

"My knee?" I asked innocently.

"Freckles," he growled, the warning clear.

"I had an accident in the parking lot at Target."

"What kind of accident?"

I decided just to get it over with. "Attempted hit and run."

"There isn't a scratch on my truck," he said, not really understanding what I meant.

"I wasn't the one doing the hitting. I was the one doing the running."

"Are you telling me someone tried to *run you over* with their car?"

"I'm fine," I insisted.

"Why didn't you call me!" he demanded.

"Because you were at work."

"So?"

"So… I'm not going to come running to you every time something happens."

"I take it you didn't call the police either?" he said, his voice tight.

"No. I just wanted to come home."

"Jesus."

"That's not very nice language."

He barked a laugh and shook his head. "You are a walking magnet for trouble."

"I didn't ask you to deal with my trouble," I snapped and then raced into the bathroom and shut myself in.

Tears burned the backs of my eyes and it made me angry. I would *not* cry. I was done crying.

I turned on the shower and then cracked the bathroom door, making sure he wasn't standing outside, just waiting to yell at me again. He wasn't, so I gathered all my things out of the bedroom and slipped back inside.

I kept the water at a lukewarm temperature; I found that hot water made me feel anxious these days—probably because of all the heat I endured in the fires. The memory of the last time I was in this shower seemed to be all I could think about.

The way his hands felt sliding over my damp skin. The way his fingers worked the shampoo through my hair and massaged the tension out of my scalp. My body began to ache for him in ways I'd never ached before. It wasn't a bad ache, though; it was the kind of ache I didn't want to go away—a deep unfurling desire that curled around beneath my skin.

I took my time washing and shaving. Thankfully, I didn't need to wash my hair and I just let the bandages on my wrists get wet. They needed changed anyway.

Once I was done, I dried and peeled away the saturated bindings, taking care to dry the wounds thoroughly. Then I opened up the bottle of peaches-and-cream body lotion and applied it to my thirsty skin, minus my wrists.

I managed to wrangle my hair into a smooth side braid that fell over my shoulder, with wispy little waves falling around my face. The only makeup I bothered with was mascara for my light lashes and some peachy-pink lip-gloss. I dressed in my sole pair of jeans and a gray T-shirt that draped across my chest.

All my bandages for my wrists were in the kitchen, and as I left the bathroom, I hoped Holt had lost some of his anger.

He was standing in the living room, but he wasn't alone. The police were here. They might as well just move in.

"Officers," I said, stepping into the room. "Is this about the man in the BMW?"

"Yes, ma'am. We were just leaving. Mr. Arkain can fill you in."

"You don't want to question me?" Surprise filtered through me.

"No need at this time," one of them replied as Holt showed them out.

He barely had the door closed when I started asking questions. "What did they say? Did they arrest that man?"

Holt strode across the room and swept me up against his chest. "I'm sorry."

The words seemed to rumble right out of his chest.

"It's okay." My voice was terribly muffled against him, so I wasn't sure if he even heard.

"It's not your fault all this is happening. I shouldn't have yelled at you."

I pulled away to get the bandages I needed. "I probably should have called you."

He took them from me and motioned for me to sit down. At this point he was used to changing these bandages and he did it on autopilot, working quickly and smoothly. "You're going to be an expert by the time these things are healed enough to be uncovered."

"It's not something I want to be an expert at," he said sadly.

A heavy silence draped around us, kind of like a thick fog in the early morning hours. "You know what I think?"

"That I'm totally awesome?"

I snorted. "Besides that."

"So you agree?"

I slapped his arm playfully. "No more talk about murder, car chases, or fire tonight."

"Don't you want to know what the cops said?"

"Not really." I was beyond tired of thinking about it all.

"So what do you suggest?"

"Dinner. Normal conversation. Ice cream."

"What about kissing?" he asked, tugging on the end of my braid.

Anticipation shot through me. "I like kissing."

"Do you like touching?" he slid his hand up the inside of my jean-clad thigh.

"Do you?" I countered boldly, doing the same to his leg.

"Careful, sweetheart. If you want to make it out of this house, watch what you do with those fingers."

Suddenly dinner didn't seem that important. "I changed my mind."

His fingers stilled where they rested on my leg. "About what?"

"I don't really need dinner." My fingers climbed a little higher. "Or conversation."

He groaned and grabbed me by the waistband of my jeans and pulled me closer so I was caught between his legs.

"All I thought about today was last night," he murmured, pulling my mouth down against his.

His tongue didn't waste any time delving into my all-too-willing mouth and stroking against mine. Lazily, our tongues spun in a circle in a seductive little dance that shot little jots of thrill down into the nerves beneath my jeans.

The muscles in my vagina began to flex like they were preparing for something… or possibly inviting something.

"Holt," I said breathless, a little bit of hesitation finding its way into the cloud of my desire.

"We're not going to do anything you don't want to do, Freckles." His hands slid up to cup my face tenderly and his kiss became achingly gentle. It was his gentleness that made me feel bold.

I climbed into his lap, straddling his waist and pressing my chest to his. It was delicious, the way his body felt beneath mine, the way every part of me became sensitized and every touch rocked me to my core.

I grasped fistfuls of his shirt and pulled it up over his back and then ran my fingers down over his bare skin. He released my face to pull the shirt up over his head and when he leaned back to kiss me again, I shook my head.

"It's my turn," I reminded him.

He dropped his hands between us, resting dangerously close to the fly of my jeans, and my body reacted, pushing itself a little closer to his hands.

He began to playfully tug at the button of my jeans as I began my exploration of his incredible physique. I started at his shoulders, splaying my hands out over their incredible mass and then trailing down lower to grip his defined biceps. His skin was smooth and warm to the touch, making me want to climb inside him and find somewhere to rest.

Keeping my grip secure, I leaned in and pressed a kiss to the corner of his lips. He turned his head so I could kiss him fully, but I pulled back and then began kissing my way to his ear, taking the lobe into my mouth and gently suckling it. When I released it, I traced my tongue upward around the shape of his ear before whispering how much I loved the way he smelled.

His hands gripped the inside of my thighs, a low groan vibrating his chest.

I glanced down, noting that my nipples weren't the only ones to have tightened into tiny little buds, so I brushed against them, stopping to pinch them lightly between my thumb and forefingers.

I glanced at him, my tongue wetting my lips. "Can I kiss you?"

"Honey, you can do whatever the hell you want."

I bent, flicking my tongue over one of those rock-hard pebbles and then covering it with my lips completely. I sucked him into my mouth and his hands found my head, tilting it so I was even closer and pinning me there. I increased the pressure, sucking a little harder, and was rewarded with a heavy moan.

Next, I slid over and did the same thing to the other as my hands began to trace around the waistband of his jeans.

When I was done lavishing his pecs with attention, I sat up, rocking forward to kiss his lips, but my movement sent an intense rush of pleasure through my center and a little gasp broke my lips.

He stared at me through heavy-lidded eyes, giving me a knowing smile. Gripping my hips, he guided me into a gentle rocking motion that proceeded to drive me half out of my mind. The way my jeans rubbed against his made me hungry, hungrier than I'd ever been.

I wound my arms around his neck, pressing myself against him, taking the lead and kissing him deeply. I didn't lift my mouth from his; I didn't come up for air. I didn't need oxygen; I needed him more.

His hands snaked between us and he used a single finger to stroke upward on the seam of my jeans that pressed against my crotch.

Something exploded within me and I groaned. I couldn't sit up straight and I collapsed against his chest as he applied more pressure against that secret spot. Wave after wave of ecstasy rolled over me, and every single coherent thought fled my mind.

When he finally pulled his hand away and slid it beneath my shirt and up my back, my body was completely boneless and flushed from head to toe. The hard ridge in his pants still pressed against me, stirring even more desire within me.

It was incredible.

I pulled back to look into his passion-laced eyes. "Take me to bed, Holt."

"If you're not ready—" he began, and I silenced his words with a provocative kiss and rocked against him once more.

He stood as I locked my legs around his waist and he carried me into the bedroom, yanking the covers down and draping me across the center of the mattress.

I sat up, reaching for the button on his jeans.

His hand covered mine. "Are you sure?"

I had never been so sure of anything in my entire life. In fact, I was sure if he didn't cover his body with mine right then and there, I would go insane.

"Have you ever wanted something so badly that you could barely see?" I whispered.

"Every single day since you walked into this house."

I brushed his hand away and unfastened his jeans, slowly lowering the zipper. With a gentle tug, he gave in, abandoning them to the floor. My eyes trained directly at the bulge beneath his boxer briefs. It was a very large bulge that made me swallow thickly.

He pushed me backward onto the bed, leaning over me, and his erection brushed against the inside of my thigh. I wondered again about its size, but before I could worry, he was moving down to grasp the end of my jeans at my ankles. The fabric of the jeans scraped over my legs as he tugged them away and the cool air of the bedroom brushed against my overheated skin.

When my pants were gone, he lifted up my foot and began kissing down the inside of my leg. I started to tremble with desire. It was almost as if my body understood what it was going to do and it urged me on, barely able to contain its thrill.

His kiss was at the back of my knee now, moving down... down... so he nipped at the inside of my thigh. I looked down the length of my body at the striking contrast of his dark head against the paleness of my thigh. I shivered.

"Holt," I said, shocked by the deep rasp in my tone.

He glanced up, those light eyes piercing me from just above my most secret place. I thought he might say something.

He didn't.

With our eyes locked, I watched as he licked up the center of my panties. My back arched up off the bed and an involuntary moan pierced the silence around us.

He hooked his fingers in the fabric and slid it down my legs, tossing it somewhere over his shoulder. Then he leaned back down, nuzzling the soft folds of my center, and began to do things with his tongue that were utterly sinful.

In between gasps, I felt his fingers gently part my folds and then the slightly rough texture of his tongue delved into my entrance and made me cry out.

I grabbed up fistfuls of the sheets on either side of my hips and squeezed them until I thought the fabric might rip. My knees were shaking so uncontrollably that I probably would have been embarrassed if I had room for thought inside my brain.

Just before I tumbled once again over the edge of complete bliss, he pulled back and smiled. "You're so incredibly wet and you taste so sweet."

I sat up, my head swimming a little like I was drunk, and reached for the waistband of his boxers. He was so hard now that it created a tent.

Before pulling the fabric down, I leaned forward and pressed a trail if kisses down his abdomen and beneath his belly button.

Holt pulled my shirt up over my head and reached around to unclasp my bra, leaving me completely naked to his eyes. It was only fair that he become as bare as I.

I stripped away the last remaining barrier between us, my eyes widening at the way he jutted upward into the space.

It was the first time I'd ever seen this part of a man in person. I wanted to touch it, to see what kind of reaction he would have, but I was afraid he wouldn't like it. I was afraid I would do it wrong.

I decided to start at the inside of his thighs, the way he did to me. The skin here wasn't as smooth as his upper body. Hair covered the tops of his legs and grew thickly just above his penis.

As I went up, I cupped his balls in my hand, gently brushing my thumb in an even circle around them before giving them a very gentle squeeze and moving on.

I glanced up at him, again unsure, but his eyes were closed and his breathing was labored, so I assumed I was doing it right.

With that little bit of encouragement, I wrapped my hand around the base of his hardness and gently stroked upward. This was the silkiest, softest part on his entire body. The head was a little bit wider than the rest, and as I slid upward, my hand caught just beneath it and he jerked, a moan ripping from his chest.

"Are you trying to kill me?" Holt said, his voice strained.

"What? No." I pulled my hand away, thinking I'd done something wrong.

He made a sound and pushed me back on the bed, coming over me, his weight pinning me to the mattress.

"You didn't do anything wrong, Freckles. You did everything so perfectly that if I allow you to touch me anymore, the fun will be over before it begins."

I reached up and ran a hand against his soft beard, enjoying the way it tickled my palm.

"I'll be right back," he said, giving me a quick kiss before disappearing into his adjoining bathroom. I took the opportunity to slide up onto the bed, placing my head near the pillows.

Several seconds later, he reappeared with a small foil packet in his hand. He tossed it beside me and lay down on the bed.

I kind of thought this would be the part where we—you know—did it. But I was wrong. He started kissing me again, paying attention to every single part of me like I was something that needed to be cherished.

I snuck in some touches and caresses myself, but for the most part, he wouldn't let me touch him, saying there would be plenty of time for that later.

Eventually, he settled between my still-trembling legs, the length of him teasing my entrance. He kissed me, and then I heard the tearing of the foil pack and his hands left me completely.

Before settling against me again, he placed his hands on the insides of my thighs and pushed my legs open wide. Using two of his fingers, he gently slid into my core, making me groan in anticipation.

"You're ready for me," he said softly, pulling out and then coming over me once more. "I'll be gentle," he swore.

Nerves tightened my body a little, and I grabbed on to his hips, waiting for the pain I knew was supposed to come.

"Look at me, Katie," he demanded, and so I did.

He was gorgeous and there was so much emotion swirling in his face that I cupped his jaw and pressed a kiss to his lips.

He joined our bodies in one swift motion.

I cried out, not because it hurt—though it did just a little—but because the sensation of him filling me almost sent me over the edge.

He held himself still, holding his weight above me with shaking arms.

I kissed his shoulder. I kissed his neck. I turned my head and kissed his bicep. He started to move then, tentative slow movements at first, but then they began to grow.

"Tell me you're okay," he whispered in my ear.

"I'm perfect."

He pulled out and then plunged into me again and again, completely rocking my entire world. Tension began to build within me, and I started to move with him, seeking sweet release.

Holt dipped his head and drew one of my nipples into his mouth, scrapping over it with his teeth.

I cried out, my entire body shuddering as a powerful orgasm ripped through me. I grabbed hold of him, hanging on, afraid I might spin away.

Above me his body went rigid and with one final plunge, I felt his release in my center. His hardness jerked again and again, stroking against the walls of my cervix.

"Holy fuck," he said after a few minutes of nothing but our heavy breathing. He rolled off of me, collapsing onto the bed and staring at the ceiling. "That was…" His words died away.

"Was it okay?" I asked, my body singing. It had never been so satisfied, ever. I just hoped he felt the same.

He laughed. "That right there was every man and boy's wet dream come to life."

I guess that meant it was good.

He rolled onto his side and placed a hand against my head. "What about you? Feel okay?"

I heard the slightest bit of self-doubt in his tone, and I smiled. "This right here was the best first time any girl or woman has ever had."

He grinned. He had a really good grin.

"Who's the man?" he sang.

"You are definitely the man," I said, laughing.

He gave me a quick kiss and then bounded into the bathroom, where I heard the water run and the toilet flush. I knew I needed to clean myself up as well, but I couldn't find the energy to get out of bed. Holt returned, still completely naked, but this time his, um… parts weren't standing at attention.

He was carrying a small white cloth and he climbed between my legs and proceeded to clean me up. "You don't have to do that," I said, suddenly feeling very shy.

"It's my job to take care of you," he said, no hint of challenge in his voice. It was as if he appointed himself my sole caretaker and it was the most important job he would ever have.

Suddenly it didn't seem like such a bad thing to be taken care of by Holt.

When he was done cleaning me up, he tossed the cloth into the bathroom where it smacked against the tile floor. He stretched out alongside me, gathered me into his arms, and rested his chin atop my head.

I lifted my head and looked down at him through the very dim lighting. "Will you let me take care of you, too?"

His face softened and he smiled. "Yeah."

I settled back against him, feeling a gentle swelling in my chest.

After a few moments, he said, "So how are you going to take care of me?"

I slid my hand across his stomach and down toward his hips. His chest rumbled with pleasure, but he caught my hand. "Not so fast there. Your body is going to need a little time to adjust."

"I feel fine," I grumbled, and then my stomach growled loudly.

"Sounds to me like someone needs to eat."

"How about ice cream?"

"Ice cream it is," he said, patting the side of my hip.

"And after the ice cream?"

"I think it's going to be past your bedtime. I'm going to have to tuck you in." His hand moved to my breast as he spoke.

"Promise?"

"Oh, sweetheart, do I ever."

17

I can't believe I just did that. Okay, that was a completely juvenile thought and so was the fact that I grabbed up my clothes and hurried into the bathroom only to lean against the back of the door and grin like an idiot while butterflies completely took over the inside of my body.

I suppressed a light giggle and began to dress in my olive-green T-shirt dress. One glance in the mirror told me I had total bedhead. I released the rumpled braid and combed through the now wavy locks.

I just lost my virginity. And it was incredible.

I never realized sex could feel like that. Just thinking about it, my body practically slid into a puddle right there on the floor. Everything inside me felt loose and liquid. My head was slightly tipsy like I had one too many glasses of wine. I was also more aware of my feminine parts, more so than I'd ever been before. I felt different down there—stretched, slightly sore, and maybe even a little swollen.

I put down the comb and looked at myself in the mirror—straight in the eyes. Did I have regrets? I searched within myself; I dug deep, past the tingling of my body, the satisfaction within my limbs. I looked hard, not shying away from any of the thoughts and feelings swirling around inside me.

And I found the answer.

No.

Well, okay, maybe I did have one regret: the fact that I hadn't done this sooner.

Another little giggle slipped out of my mouth and I grabbed up my lip-gloss, coating my lips. Holt knocked on the bathroom door as he moved down the hallway. "Get your butt out here, Freckles. You look hot."

I take that back.

I'm glad I hadn't done this sooner. I'm glad I took my time and waited for someone who actually made me feel this way. I might be inexperienced when it came to sex and romance, but I knew not every woman experienced this. In fact, I was almost positive there was no one else that could ever make me feel the way Holt did.

After carefully washing my hands, I walked out to the living room, grabbing up my bag and shoving my feet into my flip-flops. Holt held open the door for me and we stepped out into the late-evening sun.

Just when my feet stepped into the grass, a silver BMW pulled into the driveway and parked behind Holt's truck.

I froze, not really sure what to do. Shouldn't this guy be in jail? Shouldn't he be sitting at the police station for what he tried to do to me just hours ago?

Couldn't a girl go get ice cream without worrying about who might be waiting for her outside?

Holt moved up beside me, palming his keys, looking toward the BMW with irritation written all over his face. I thought it was a little strange he wasn't displaying the murderous feelings he claimed to feel for this guy earlier.

Wonder why…

"Now might be a good time to tell me what the cops said."

He placed his hand at the small of my back and angled his body toward me and slightly forward. "He's a lawyer. He claims he's been trying to talk to you for a while now."

"So lawyers usually try to run people off the road when they want to talk?" I snorted. "People have these things now called phones."

"You don't have a phone anymore," he reminded me gently.

Oh. Well, there was that.

But I still wasn't willing to give this guy the benefit of the doubt. He scared me.

"The cops couldn't hold him. Technically, he didn't do anything wrong." He spoke quietly, leaning in to softly say the words near my ear.

"You believe them?" I asked, turning to look into his eyes.

I saw the cloud of doubt that shadowed the blue. "I certainly don't plan on trusting him. But maybe we should at least ask him before I unleash the mad dog."

I arched an eyebrow. "The mad dog?"

He grinned. "Inside every man there is a mad dog just waiting to get out."

"Right." I would just file that under useless information that I would never need to know again.

Mr. BMW opened up his car door and stepped out, standing between his car and the door to stare at us over the roof. "Miss Parker? I apologize for the misunderstanding earlier, but my name is Paul Goddard, from Goddard, Goldberg, and Stein. I'm an attorney. I've come a long way to speak to you."

Was this just some lame attempt at getting close enough to kill me?

Holt leaned down and whispered in my ear, "The cops said his identity checks out."

"What do you want?" I called to the man.

"I just need a few minutes of your time. It's about some legal documents."

"Is this about my house burning down?"

"No, ma'am. I wasn't aware your house burned down until I arrived in town today."

"Where are you from?"

"Hollywood, California."

"I don't know anyone in California."

"Would it be okay if I came closer to explain?"

I pondered that request for a moment. He was certainly being cautious this time around. He did look like a lawyer. Wearing a dark suit and tie. His salt-and-pepper hair was short and he had a deep tan, which implied he could be from California (either that or he had an unhealthy addiction to the tanning bed).

Of course, now I was curious as to what this could possibly be about.

"Okay," I told him.

He reached in his car and grabbed a briefcase, shut his door, and walked across the yard to stand a few feet away. He had a black eye from where one of the men at the fire station punched him. I didn't feel bad about it. He deserved it.

"I feel we've gotten off on the wrong foot," he began.

I laughed. "If you consider following me through Wilmington, tailgating my car, and trying to run me off the road 'getting off on the wrong foot,' then I suppose you're right."

"I wasn't trying to run you off the road. I was trying to get your attention. You are a very hard woman to find, Miss Parker."

"You called me Katie before."

"Again, another mistake. I thought you might stop panicking if I called you by your first name. I thought it would give you the impression I was familiar with you."

Holt snorted. "Familiar like a stalker."

"Yes, well." He cleared his throat. "I hadn't realized you were having some… trouble until I was escorted to the police station."

I crossed my arms over my chest. "Someone's trying to kill me," I replied bluntly.

"I'm afraid I might know the reason why."

Holt stiffened beside me and I gripped my purse, twisting the strap in my hands. "Maybe we should talk about this inside."

Holt handed me the keys to the front door and then ushered me ahead of him, keeping himself between me and the lawyer at all times.

I perched on the end of the couch, anxiety and suspicion cloaking me. Holt sat down beside me and I slid a glance at him. "Did the police say anything about this to you?" I asked out of the side of my lips.

He gave a faint shake of his head.

Mr. Goddard heard and replied, "I didn't discuss this with the police. Attorney-client privileges."

"I'm not your client." I was getting irritated with all of this talk I didn't understand.

"No. But your father was."

You could have heard a pin drop in the silence that followed. I shifted uncomfortably. "You must be mistaken. I don't have a father."

"Miss Parker, do you know who Tony Diesel was?"

I wrinkled my nose, thinking back to the commercial I saw earlier. "The rock singer?"

"Don't tell me you don't like rock," Holt said.

"It's not my favorite."

He put a hand over his heart like I shot him and made a face.

I rolled my eyes.

"Tony Diesel was like a rock god," Holt announced. "Such a shame about his death."

I looked back at Mr. Goddard, who was shaking his head solemnly. "What does this have to do with anything?"

"Mr. Diesel named you in his Last Will and Testament."

"Me?" I said, feeling more confused by the second.

"You are Katherine Eileen Parker, are you not?"

"I go by Katie."

"You were born on March 15, 1991, and your mother's name is Elena Marie Parker."

"Was," I corrected, my voice hollow.

"Excuse me?"

"My mother died several years ago."

"I'm sorry, I only know the information that was on file. I didn't look into your… situation. I really should have."

"Don't apologize. It's fine."

Mr. Goddard paused, sitting down on the opposite end of the couch and glancing at Holt as he did so. When Holt didn't object, he laid his briefcase on the space between us and opened it, reaching in to grab a stack of bound papers.

Then he looked up.

"Tony Diesel named you as his sole surviving relative—his daughter, to be precise."

I jerked like someone slapped me and stared at him so intently that my vision went blurry. Holt slipped an arm around my waist, but I scarcely felt it.

"He was not my father," I whispered, pain slicing through my chest. If this was some kind of sick joke, it was very, very mean.

"In all honesty, I don't know if he is or not. But he seemed to think you were. I have here a letter—a letter written by Elena Parker dated in the fall of 1990. She wrote to your father, explaining that she was pregnant, that he was the father." As he spoke, he handed me the letter.

I unfolded it, staring down at the handwriting that belonged to my mother. I stared at it, feeling tears well in my eyes as I traced with my finger the letters—the words—that she wrote. My mother once held this piece of paper. The sentences written here were all thoughts that were inside her brain. Throughout the last seven years, I lost pieces of her, pieces that I still mourned but pieces that I would never get back. What little I did have burned the night of my house fire.

This letter… it represented so much. It was the last remaining piece of the only person I ever loved.

"Hey," Holt said softly, running his hand over the back of my hair.

"Can I keep this?" I asked, looking at Mr. Goddard.

"Yes." Then he slid the packet of papers—a will—over toward me. "I know this must be incredibly difficult to hear. Tony Diesel… well, if I may be frank?"

"Please," I said, still gazing at the letter as a single tear tracked over my cheek.

"Tony Diesel was a brilliant musician. He never missed a show, loved his fans, and worked hard at his job."

"I sense a but coming on," Holt said.

"But he was also selfish, a drug addict, and could be a real bastard."

"And?" I prompted.

"And, so he ignored your mother and this letter completely. He never acknowledged you as his daughter until he came into my offices with that letter a couple years ago and said he wanted to leave the bulk of his estate to you."

"Why would he do that?"

"My guess? Because he didn't have any other family and the friends he had were all very wealthy." He paused. "And because he liked to cause a stir. He likely wanted to shock people one final time."

"Well, I'm definitely shocked."

"I brought the documents with me for you to sign."

"What if I'm not really his daughter?"

The lawyer paused and looked up. "I'm afraid that with him and your mother gone, you might not ever know for sure. But it really doesn't matter."

"It doesn't?" Holt asked, sitting forward.

"No. Legally this money is yours."

"And you think this is the reason someone wants to kill me?"

"I think it's quite possible."

"How much money are you talking about here?" Holt asked.

"Forty million dollars."

Holt whistled between his teeth and sat back against the cushions. "That's a pretty legit motive for murder."

I couldn't even comprehend that amount of money. It was more than any one person could ever need. "What if I don't want it?" I said, the thought blurting from my mouth.

"Well, you could donate it all to charity."

I nodded. I could do that. I could sign it all away and then never have to think about any of this ever again.

"Miss Parker, take some time to think about it. This isn't something that needs to be decided overnight. The money can sit in the bank until you know for sure what you want to do."

"Did he have a home? Cars?" Holt asked.

"Yes, he had several homes. All of them but one will be put up for sale. That money is yours as well."

"What will happen to the one that isn't for sale?"

"He actually left that to someone else."

"I thought you said he didn't have any other family."

"He doesn't. He left it to his latest ex-wife. She lived there briefly, so I suppose he felt it was partly hers."

"How long were they married?" I asked.

"Only a year. They divorced two years ago."

We all sat there in awkward silence for several long moments before Mr. Goddard cleared his throat. "I'm going to leave a copy of the will and testament and several other documents for you to look over. My flight back to California isn't until the day after tomorrow. Take a night to sleep on it, and we can meet again tomorrow."

He piled some papers on the center of the couch and then closed up his briefcase. He stood, stared at me, then sat back down.

"Is there something else?" Holt said, leaning forward again.

"I feel I should warn you," he began.

"About?" I questioned.

"I wasn't your fath—Tony's lawyer. I didn't handle any of his legal issues except this will. As I said, he came to me a few years ago with that letter and he asked me to draw up a new will, which I did."

"What about his other lawyer?"

"He is an associate at my firm. His name is William Courtland and he worked with Tony for twenty years. He was on retainer and handled all of Tony's personal and professional business. They were friends as well. I always told him mixing friendship with business was a bad idea, but he maintained that it wasn't a problem."

"And he didn't know Tony came to you to change his will?"

"I don't think so. I never told him, and it seems to me if Tony wanted him to know about the changes, he would have had William make them." As he spoke, a fine sheen of sweat broke out across his upper lip and he swiped at his forehead with the back of his hand. I couldn't figure out why this would make him so anxious. But then he continued.

"We haven't spoken to William in over two weeks. The last meeting we had, he was preparing the documents to fly them out here to notify you and get your signatures. I'm assuming he never arrived?"

"No."

He frowned, his thoughts turning inward. It was obvious this man's disappearance bothered him.

"Has he ever done anything like this before?" Holt asked.

"No." Then he shrugged. "Well, yes, but he was usually with Tony and he always called in to notify us." Then he looked Holt directly in the eye. "It feels different this time."

Holt nodded slowly.

"Different how?" I asked, frustrated that they seemed to be having some sort of unspoken conversation.

"William was angry when found out the bulk of Tony's estate was left to you. He felt after twenty years of loyal friendship, of being on call for Tony twenty-four hours a day, he deserved some sort of compensation."

"Tony didn't leave him anything?" I asked, thinking how terrible that was.

"He did. Several million dollars. But William didn't seem to think that was enough." Again, he looked at Holt.

"Why would you ask him to bring the documents if he was angry?"

Again, Mr. Goddard wiped at his brow. "Because he seemed to accept the will after a few days. He went to the private funeral. He came to work every day. When I had an important client meeting, he offered to bring the documents. He said it could be his last official case for Tony."

So basically, what he was saying was out there somewhere—somewhere likely nearby—was a man who felt betrayed and shoved aside and all of that anger was directed at me.

Forty million dollars didn't seem like a good enough reason for me to die.

"Thank you for coming by," Holt said, standing up. Mr. Goddard did the same and the two men walked over to the door.

I followed but stopped beside the couch, needing some space. "I'm sorry about having you arrested. And for your eye," I said. I still wasn't sorry for the way I acted. I felt threatened; I had a right to feel that way, and I was just reacting to my situation.

"You have my sincere apologies, Miss Parker. I truly did not mean to scare you."

He pulled a business card out of the inside of his jacket and extended it to Holt. "Here's my card. You can reach me by my cell phone. I'm staying at the Hampton Inn here in Wilmington. Call me tomorrow to arrange a time for us to meet again."

Holt replied and then showed him out. I stood there numbly staring at my toes. My mind was going in so many different directions; I couldn't really settle on any single thought. Instead, the inside of my brain sounded like there were a hundred different people all whispering, all trying to talk at once.

I made my way around the side of the couch and sat down, letting my hands fall between my knees. The walls of this house felt like they were caving in, like there was this pressure pushing me from all sides.

I had a father.
Maybe.
He was a drug addict.
He was dead.
He left me forty million dollars.

But the one thought that seemed to scream louder than most?

My mother never told me.

Holt stepped in front of me, holding out his hand for me to take. I looked up, leaving his hand suspended between us.

"Come on, you need to get out of here."

"Where will we go?"

"You'll see."

18

It was fully dark by the time we arrived at our destination. We rolled down the windows, and warm night air, heavy with the scent of salt and the sea, wafted into the cab and surrounded us.

I was surprised when he pulled into a very bright roadside store and disappeared inside for a few minutes before returning and driving a short distance to a public access spot on the beach.

"I hope you like the beach," he said, seeming to suddenly second-guess his decision to bring me here.

"I love the beach."

He smiled and reached into a brown paper sack. When he withdrew his hand, he was holding a popsicle, one of the classic kinds shaped like a rocket ship with layers of red, white, and blue.

"It's not ice cream, but…" Even if I hated popsicles, I would have taken it and enjoyed it just because of the look on his face. He looked like a little boy who was excited for Christmas morning, or a rat who'd outsmarted a trap and ran away with the cheese.

But I happened to love popsicles. So I didn't have to pretend the squeal of delight I made while I unwrapped it and slid my lips around the icy, sweet top.

"Mmmm," I said as I licked at the flavors.

He watched me, his eyes turning heated.

"Want some?" I held it out toward him. He leaned forward and wrapped his lips around it the same way I had just seconds before.

He stared at me intently as he drew back, sucking the sweetness as he went.

Pinpricks of desire raced along my skin. "Did you get one?" I asked, my voice taking on a throaty quality.

He reached into the sack and pulled out one identical to mine.

I snatched mine away. "Hey! Eat your own, then."

He chuckled as we exited the truck with our icy treats and walked to the wooden stairs and long plank-like walkway that led down to the sand.

Even though it was dark, the ocean was still a gorgeous sight. We stood side-by-side just looking out at the sweeping view. It was an endless sea of dark waves capped with white that crashed along the shoreline and rushed toward the beach. White foam floated along the mysterious water, buoyant and free.

The moon had risen just above the water's edge in the distance and it hung low, heavy, and full, shining a brilliant shade of gold. It reflected off the surface of the water, highlighting a section of the never-still ocean.

The wind blew off the water, and I closed my eyes and inhaled, feeling my hair lifting off my shoulders and dancing behind me as I took in the heady scent that only nature at its best could produce.

Holt slipped his fingers into mine, linking us together and easily leading me down the steps and onto the sand. I kicked off my flip-flops, eager to delve my toes into the gritty softness of the sand. It was still slightly warm from the day's sun.

I loved the way it crowded around my toes and buried the tops of my feet. Holt took off his sandals too and we placed them on the bottom step and wandered closer to the water's edge.

We didn't say anything as we strolled, hand in hand, down the lonely stretch of beach. The sound of the surf filled the silence and the lack of people made me feel as if we were the only two people in the world.

I lifted my chin, gazing up at the millions of stars shining in the sky. Stars always looked more brilliant when standing on a beach. It was because the land here wasn't interrupted by buildings and businesses, by lights and music. It was darker here, tranquil.

"I needed this," I told him, catching the tail end of a falling star.

"The beach has a way of making a person feel small," he replied.

He was exactly right. That's exactly why I felt better. Because out here, staring out at this giant body of water, at the endless amount of sky, I did feel small—like there was so much more out there than I realized. At home earlier, all I could feel and think about were the problems, the way my life seemed to be caving in. Things seemed so large and insurmountable. I felt like I might never get out from under them.

But not here.

Here I felt like I could breathe. I felt like the wind coming off the waves was carrying away the worst of my worries and the water was going to soak up the worst of my pain. Out here I didn't feel like my entire world was crumbling. It was here I realized how lucky I was just to... *be*.

"Your popsicle's going to melt," Holt said, leaning down to whisper in my ear.

A large wave crashed against the shore and rushed forward, soaking our feet and making me laugh. "It's cold!" I squealed, trying to get out of its way and failing.

Holt released my hand to wrap an arm around my waist and lift me up so my feet dangled above the water.

My chest was pressed against his as he towed me along, backtracking out of the waves. I clung to him, laughing, afraid he would drop me and I would plunge into the chilly inch of water.

When we were farther up on the dry sand, he stopped, staring into my eyes while my stomach somersaulted. He closed the mere inches between us, pressing his voluptuous lips against mine in a warm and lingering kiss.

Then he released me to sit in the sand, spreading his legs wide and motioning for me to sit between them. I did, pressing my back to his front and stretching my legs out along with his. I giggled when I saw that my feet only made it to his mid-calves.

I hadn't realized how cold my skin had turned until he wrapped both arms around me. It was like stepping into a ray of sun on a cold and windy day. His chin rested on the crown of my head and I could feel thin strands of my hair stick to the scruffy area of his jaw.

I concentrated on the dripping treat in my hand, trying not to slurp it too loudly, but then finally giving up and just digging in. When it was gone, I used the stick to trace uneven patterns in the sand between our legs.

"Katie, will you tell me about you?" He spoke closely into my ear so the wind wouldn't carry away his words before I could hear them.

I leaned into him a little farther, enjoying the feeling of being completely surrounded by him, and tilted my head back, angling it so my words were directed toward him.

"It was just me and my mom for most of my life," I began, feeling a little awkward because this was the very first time I ever told anyone about my past.

"She never told me who my father was, only that he wasn't interested in being a father and that I was better off without him anyway. When I was fifteen years old, she was killed in a car accident." Holt's embrace tightened around me, but he didn't say anything or interrupt my words.

"We didn't have any other family. My entire life had been just her and me. So when she died, I was sent into the system, into foster care. I tried to get emancipated, but the judge said I was too young to live on my own."

I paused to glance back out at the rolling waves, still using the stick to trace in the sand.

"I moved a lot, usually at least once a year. Sometimes three times a year. There were a couple

nice foster families, but the rest seemed like they were
tired and wrung out from the system. I don't know
why they continued to foster kids when they clearly
were so tired of it. I guess it was for the money, or
maybe they just didn't know how to tell the
government they were tired of babysitting. It seemed
like every time I moved, I had to give up more and
more of my life before Mom died. Keeping all my
possessions became a pain to move around and lots
of times I didn't have my own room to keep them in
anyway."

"That sounds like it was hard."

"It wasn't the material possessions that were hard
to give, but the memories that were attached to
them."

I felt him nod against my head and I continued.
"I was shuffled around, lost in the system for three
years. I worked everywhere I went. I took on as many
hours as I could. I read constantly. Books were my
greatest companion and stories my greatest
distraction. I saved every penny I had, hoping one day
I would be able to have my own life, my own house,
somewhere that no one could ever take it away."

"The day I turned eighteen, I walked out of my
final foster home with a couple suitcases to my name.
I went to college on a scholarship and lived in a tiny
apartment, still working and trying to save. I didn't
bother to get close to people or make any friends. But
I love books, I love literature, and I love the quietness
of the inside of a library, so I became a librarian."

"You didn't make any friends? Not even one?"

"Not even one," I replied, tilting my head back
to look up at him.

"My father never wanted to know me and my mother left me. I know she hadn't wanted to leave me that way, but it still left a gaping hole in my life. The people in the foster system always sort of looked *through* me instead of *at* me. And so I decided I would rather spend my time with fictional characters than real-life ones."

"That sounds real lonely, Freckles."

I loved the way his chest rumbled when he talked. It vibrated against my back.

"I was happy," I said with a small shrug. "I had built a pretty good savings by the time I graduated college. And with the money my mother left me when she died, I was able to buy my house." I smiled a little to myself. "It was a nice house. Yellow siding and flowers in the yard. It even had a pool." I looked up at him. "You remember the pool? It was the one you threw me in."

He laughed.

"Anyway, I finally had somewhere that was mine that no one could take away." I fell silent, thinking about the charred remains there today.

"But someone did," Holt said, a hard edge coming into his voice.

"Yeah."

"So what do you think about Tony Diesel?" As he spoke, he rubbed his palm along my bare arm, almost as if his touch would make his words easier to hear.

It did.

"I don't know what to think. I suppose it's possible. I mean, Mr. Goddard said he wasn't interested in being a father and that's exactly what my mother told me."

"He left you a hell of a pile of money."

"I can't understand why. Is it some sort of apology for ignoring me my entire life? Was it because he felt guilty? If I take the money, then it would be like saying the way he behaved was okay."

"What else?" he asked, inviting me to spill more.

"Why wouldn't she tell me?" I whispered, the words ripping from the deepest part of me. That's the part that hurt the most. Feeling like my mother lied, like she withheld information that I deserved to know. She was my best friend; she was the one person I trusted over everyone else.

"Maybe she thought if she did, you would only be hurt."

"He's not even listed on my birth certificate," I said. Sadness and anger fought within me. Anger for not knowing if any of this was true and for being kept in the dark. But sadness, too, because I didn't want to feel this way. I didn't want to think negative thoughts about a woman who spent her whole life taking care of me and then died far too soon. Her memory deserved more than my anger.

"You wanna know what I think?"

I sat up and turned, tucking my knees into my chest and fitting my body between his thighs. "Tell me."

"I think the real loss is his. Whoever he is. Anyone who passes up the chance to have their life touched by you is an idiot. And I never had the chance to meet your mother, but I know she was amazing because she raised you."

I rested my chin atop my knees and smiled. "You make it sound so easy."

He shrugged. "From where I'm sitting, it seems that way."

"Would you take the money?"

He pursed his lips, then grinned. "Probably."

"Money changes people. It changes things."

"You're not one for change, are you?"

I shook my head. "No. I like stability. I like to know what to expect."

"Seems like you always expect the worst out of people," Holt said, his voice sounding very wise.

I wanted to deny it. But I couldn't because it was true.

"Ever wonder what would happen if you expected something good out of someone?" The wind blew as he spoke, and instead of carrying his words away, it brought them closer, wrapping them around my head. Around my heart.

"Not until recently."

He moved quickly, shooting forward and grasping me, tumbling us backward so I was lying across his chest and he was lying in the sand.

Most of my body was across his, with the bottom part of my legs and feet still in the sand between his legs. I rested my arms on his chest and leaned down, initiating a deep and thrusting kiss. His hand wrapped around the back of my head, holding it in place, keeping me from breaking the kiss. Like I would.

His tongue was incredible, the way it seemed to find all the secret spots inside my mouth that unlocked my desire like some ancient, magical key. Our tongues twisted so fiercely together, so deeply into the each other's mouths, I had trouble knowing where one stopped and the other began. One of my hands gripped a fistful of his T-shirt and the other found the hem and slid up between the fabric and his skin.

He was warm, the kind of warm that made my toes curl in the sand, the kind of warm that an electric blanket radiated in the dead of winter and made you reluctant to crawl out of bed. I snuggled in a little closer, wiggling against him, and a groan erupted from the back of his throat.

His hand left the back of my head and cupped my butt, pressing me ever farther against him, grinding his throbbing erection against the flimsy fabric of my dress.

I wiggled some more, liking the way it felt to rub up against him. And then the cool night air was brushing against my upper thighs, gliding against skin that had previously been covered. Holt was slipping my dress up around my hips and guiding my legs so I straddled his lap, the hard ridge in his jeans pressed firmly against my dampening panties.

I looked down at him, my hair blowing over my shoulders and hiding some of my face. I felt like there was a giant bubbling volcano inside me and it was on the verge of erupting with insanely hot lava.

He caressed the inside of my thigh with his hand, whispering to me about how silky smooth my skin felt against his. And then his hands began to move higher, sliding up beneath my dress all the way up to cup my breast, yanking down the soft cups of my bra and pinching my nipple lightly, rolling it between his fingers.

I cried out. The sensation was incredible as I began to rock my hips against him.

His other hand joined the one already up my dress and he fondled me, pinching and teasing until I thought I might go mad with need. I felt like I was going up a hill, going up and up and up and all I wanted to see was the crest—the peak of the hill—so I could go plunging right back down.

His hands drifted away from my breasts and I leaned down to kiss him, but he gently pushed me back up. His fingers found the edges of my panties, slipping inside and into the wet and ready folds.

"Holt," I whispered, my voice shaky and weak.

"Come for me, sweetness," he purred as his fingers began to move, sliding in and out, up and down. I bit down on my lip and grasped ahold of his biceps.

The tension in my body was mounting and I began to move faster, more frantic against his hand. He plunged two fingers inside me and crooked them forward, like he was motioning for me across a room. And then his free hand found the little swollen bud at my center and stroked it gently.

I erupted. My body convulsed violently atop him. I threw my head back and moaned, my eyes going wide as I stared up at the star-splattered sky. My body kept twitching as waves of pleasure overcame me again and again until finally my body quieted into a gentle all-over trembling.

Holt pulled his hands away and reached for me, pulling me down into his arms where I let out a huge contented sigh.

The sound of the waves came back to my ears; the feeling of the sand on my toes had my eyes springing wide. "Oh my gosh!" I whispered, frantic, whipping my head up and looking around. "We just did that in public!"

He chuckled. "No one else is here."

"But what if there was?"

"Then they're thinking what a lucky bastard I am right about now."

I laughed and collapsed against his chest once more. The inside of my panties was so wet it was kind of uncomfortable, so I shifted and he moaned.

My eyes snapped up to his face. I might have just had an earth shattering orgasm, but he was still rock hard.

I slid my hand over the front of his jeans.

He rolled quickly, pinning me into the sand and pressing a kiss to my lips. But then he jumped up and reached down to pull me along with him. "Come on," he said.

He took off in a jog, still holding my hand, so I started to jog too. We ran toward and old pier that had partly fallen into the sea. There were no longer any lights lining it or a little shop at the end. It was just a dark, imposing structure that jutted out into the middle of the salty sea where it then disappeared.

Holt led me beneath it, far up into the sand. It provided a wealth of cover, blocking out the stars and the ocean breeze. He grabbed me by the waist and spun me around, planting his lips on mine in a kiss so hungry I felt the stirring of brand-new desire.

I reached for his pants, pulling them open and reaching inside. I wrapped my hand around him, tightening my grip, squeezing him through the fabric of his boxers.

"I want you, Katie. I want you so fucking bad right now."

I slid my hand beneath the waistband of the boxers, cupping the proof of his words. "I'm yours."

I lay down in the sand, pulling my dress up around my waist as he reached into his back pocket and pulled out a condom. I watched as he rolled it down the incredible length of his hardness and then came forward, settling between my legs. Achingly slow, he pulled my panties down, leaving them hooked around one of my ankles. He pressed a soft kiss to the inside of my thigh, and then slid up my body so his elbows rested on either side of my head.

As he brushed the hair away from my face, he kissed me softly, slowly, as if he had all the time in the world and the blood wasn't pounding through his veins like he was running a marathon.

But I could feel his heart beating. It thumped so rapidly against my chest that I smiled.

As he kissed me, he probed the entrance to my body, slipping inside easily. I felt the eyes roll back in my head as my lids drifted closed and my head rolled to the side.

He moved against me. I answered each one of his thrusts with my own until I lifted my legs and wrapped them around his waist. He hugged me tight, pulling me against him as he penetrated me over and over so deeply that my muscles clenched.

His breathing became more labored, and I knew he was about to come when he pushed up onto his arm and reached down between us, once again finding the swollen bud. He ground his fingers against it and my back arched in surprise as another orgasm flowed through me. This one wasn't as powerful as the last, like the volcano already erupted and now the warm lava was coating everything inside me.

He moaned and his own release burst forward.

Instead of rolling off me, he kissed me as he pulled out and reached down to pull my dress over my nakedness. Only then did he roll away.

After I had my panties on and he was completely redressed, he pulled me up into his arms, hugging me close. "I brought you here so you could think, not so I could take advantage of you."

"I liked it." I confided.

He drew back. "Yeah?"

Did he really not know how hot he was? "Definitely. I've never felt this way before."

"Me either," he said, taking my hand and leading me back the way we came. This time we walked closer to the water's edge so the surf could rush over our feet.

"Not even with Taylor?"

He snorted and stopped, pulling me around to look at me. "All of my feelings for Taylor were here," he said, taking my hand and rubbing it against his fly. "With you…" he said, lifting my hand and bringing it to rest over his heart. "My feelings are mostly in here."

This feeling of rightness descended upon me, like I was exactly where I was supposed to be. I swallowed past the lump lodged in my throat.

"So Taylor must have been pretty good in bed," I said, trying not to feel jealous but failing.

He rolled his eyes. "Were you just back there?" He motioned to the pier. "That was way better than 'pretty good.'"

I giggled, not knowing what else to say.

"I don't want to talk about Taylor. She's my past. You're my future."

I stopped walking as water rushed up around my ankles and tiny droplets spattered against my calves. "I am?"

"Yeah. You got a problem with that?"

I shook my head, so many feelings overwhelming me. He smiled and we started walking again.

I did want to be part of Holt's future. I wanted it more than I wanted anything. In barely any time at all, he managed to insert himself so wholly into my life that I couldn't imagine a day without him.

That scared me.

For two reasons:

One, giving away my heart meant I ran the risk of getting it broken.

And, two, with someone out there trying to kill me, I wasn't even sure I had a future.

19

I woke up in his arms with the steady sound of his heartbeat beneath my ear. I wasn't wearing a shirt and neither was he, so our skin was pressed together and my leg was tossed up over his.

I lay there for a long time, letting the ceiling fan brush my skin with cool air as my body gently moved with the even rising and falling of Holt's chest as he breathed.

I thought about my mother, my home, the fires, Mr. Goddard, and Tony Diesel. I had a lot of decisions to make, a life to put back together.

Funny thing was, even after everything, I didn't feel like my life had fallen apart.

I felt like it had fallen together.

I never really allowed myself to think outside the box before. From the age of fifteen, I decided what I wanted, set a path, and followed it. I had only one goal in mind. Stability and independence. It's all I truly wanted... but now that didn't seem like near enough.

My home was taken from me. My job put on hold. Someone tried to run me over with a car, and I moved in with a stranger.

But through it all, I learned that maybe there was more to life than my job, my home was something that could be replaced (and maybe by something even better), and I wasn't ready to die because life was finally getting interesting.

I didn't need to know for sure if Tony Diesel really was my father because it didn't matter. It wouldn't change the way I was raised, the memories I had of my mother, and I wasn't about to let it dictate my future.

I didn't have everything figured out, and I didn't know what was going to happen, but that was okay.

Beneath me, Holt stirred, so I leaned up to pepper his face with kisses. He stretched against me and then rolled, wrapping me in his arms and pinning me against the mattress. "I could get used to waking up like this," he murmured before dipping his head and kissing me.

"What time do you have to be at work?" I asked when he finally pulled away.

"I don't. I took today off."

I arched an eyebrow. "You did?"

"With everything going on, I wouldn't be able to concentrate at work anyway knowing you were here alone."

"I'm a big girl, Holt." I didn't want him thinking I couldn't take care of myself.

"Actually, you're kind of tiny."

I grabbed him by the face. "If you need to go to work, go."

"The only place I need to go is out for pancakes."

"Can I come too?" I asked sweetly, batting my eyes.

"I might be persuaded to bring you along," he said suggestively.

"Hmmmm," I replied playfully, reaching around and cupping his butt. "Well, I should probably get to work *persuading* you."

I did a really good job.

*   *   *

The waitress delivered me a plate of towering blueberry pancakes dripping in butter. The sweet scent of the fluffy goodness had my stomach rumbling in appreciation. I pushed back my tall glass of orange juice to make way for the food that was about to be introduced to my belly.

I swirled my finger around in a giant pad of softening butter and brought it to my lips as the waitress handed Holt his own stack of pancakes plus a plate loaded with scrambled eggs, bacon, and toast.

When she was gone, I reached for the syrup.

"Are you trying to kill me?" Holt said, leaning over the table and stabbing his fork in my direction.

I glanced dubiously at the fork. "Are you trying to kill me?"

He grinned. "You can't just go around licking your fingers like that, Freckles. It makes a man forget he's in a public place."

I laughed and dug into my pancakes, shoving an unladylike bite into my mouth and then groaning as the sweetness slid over my tongue.

"There you go again," he said, his eyes darkening with desire.

"Wasn't last night and this morning enough for you?" I asked playfully.

"I don't think I'll ever get enough of you."

His words affected me somehow… A sort of longing came over me. What he said implied some kind of long-standing relationship, something that would last. The idea that this could be my life, that my days could be filled with passion and laughter, was so intensely wanted that it caught me off guard.

I watched him eat for a few minutes and as I looked, I realized I didn't really know much about him other than the fact he was divorced. "So how's a guy become the fire chef at the age of twenty-four? That's kind of young, isn't it?"

"It just kind of happened."

"I'm gonna need more than that," I said, feeling brave and stealing a piece of bacon off his plate. I saw the hostess leading a woman across the room and seating her in a booth near our table. The woman had long very blond hair and lips so full I thought surely they must have been treated with Botox. I watched as she slid into the booth, took the offered menu, and ordered a coffee. There was something about her… something that seemed vaguely familiar. When the hostess disappeared, she looked up, catching me staring. I averted my gaze immediately and returned my attention to Holt.

He set his fork down and looked up. "Fire control was something that always seemed to interest me," he explained while I chomped down on the bacon. "So when I was sixteen, my dad suggested I volunteer with the local fire department. So I did and

I really liked it. The guys there were really cool and it was something I felt made a difference in people's lives."

"Sounds like you had a great dad."

He nodded. "Yeah, both my parents are really great."

"They're still married?"

"Yep, they live across town. They're going love you."

"Me?" I choked, reaching for my juice. "Why would they want to meet me?"

"They're going to want to know the reason their son is so happy."

I abandoned my food and fought the urge to cry. I didn't want to hope… I didn't want to think there might be a family—a family full of people like Holt— that would embrace me and make me one of their own. I spent too much time hoping for that with every single foster home I went to. In the end, it all turned out exactly the same way: bad.

His hand came across the table and covered mine. "Hey, what did I say?"

I shook my head. "Nothing, I just…"

"What?" he prompted when I didn't speak.

"I've just gotten really used to being alone."

He squeezed my fingers. "You're not alone anymore, Katie. You're never going to be alone again."

He pulled his hand away and went back to eating, like his words didn't just alter the entire universe.

But they did.

"So are you going to finish telling me about your job?" I said, clearing my throat and attempting to get back to a less mind-shattering conversation.

"I volunteered for years. Then when I graduated high school, I went through fire training, CPR training, basic medical training, fire safety training, and did a lot of physical work to get myself into shape. When I finished all that, the WPD called and offered me a job with them."

"You worked really hard."

"I guess when it's something you love, it doesn't feel like work."

I nodded. I understood because that's the way I felt about books.

"So when did you become the fire chief?"

His expression turned grim. "About a year ago."

I leaned farther into the table so I didn't miss anything he was about to say.

"We got called out on a nasty fire. Some old building that sat out on the edge of town. By the time we got there, the place was a wreck. The flames were so high and bright it was insane. We got to work, trying to put out the flames, but it seemed like no matter what we did, it just kept burning stronger." His eyes were far away and I could tell he was lost in the memory of that day.

"We finally managed to dim the flames on one side of the building. Most of the exterior was gone by that point so the chief and a couple guys moved in a little farther because it seemed like there was something going on we didn't quite understand. Just as they moved closer, what was left of the building exploded."

I put a hand up to my mouth, gasping lightly.

"Debris went everywhere, men went down, and the chief... he was pinned beneath a flaming piece of timber."

"Then what happened?"

"It all happened really fast. I just started moving, you know? I went on autopilot just doing what I thought needed to be done. I instructed the other men to help me drag the injured guys over by the truck and administer what first aid they could. I called for backup and an ambulance and instructed the other men to just keep spraying. I knew whatever had been inside was destroyed, so the fire might be containable at that point.

"What about the chief?"

"He was still pinned. At first I thought he was dead... but then I saw him move, little jerks of pain because he was being burned in the fire."

I remembered the overwhelming fear of thinking I was going to burn to death, of the way the smoke smothered my lungs and I thought I was going to choke and expire. I remembered the way my skin felt, the intense rush of the burn, the all-consuming pain that chased away all reason. I stared down at my bandaged wrists, imagining the horror of lying there burning, knowing the pain wouldn't stop until I was dead.

"I grabbed an extinguisher and rushed toward the worst of the flames, creating a sort of path to his body. Then I sprayed him and the beam, completely coating everything around us. I probably shouldn't have picked him up, but it was that or let the fire completely overtake him. He screamed when I touched him. It was the kind of scream I never want to hear again. Thankfully, as we were moving, he passed out."

"You saved his life," I murmured, then looked up. "He did survive, didn't he?"

"Yes, he did. He suffered extensive burns, but he lived."

"How horrible."

"When I went to see him in the hospital a few weeks later, I was a little afraid he would be mad at me for saving him. I mean, because of me he was sitting in a hospital bed covered in bandages and in the kind of pain that I wouldn't even wish on my worst enemy."

"Was he mad?"

He smiled. "When I got to his room, there was a girl about the age of ten sitting on the end of his bed, reading him a book about horses. When he saw me, he told her to go get an ice cream, and when she was gone, he…"

"He what?" I demanded.

"He thanked me. He told me even though he was in the worst pain of his entire life and he had months of recovery ahead of him, he was grateful to be alive."

"How is he today?"

"He's doing good. He's still recovering, but he's come a long way. He retired with full honor and spends a lot of time with his family now."

"So they made you fire chief," I finished for him, my heart swelling with pride.

"I didn't want the job at first, but they were persistent and the other guys they asked refused the job because they all said I earned the title."

"You did."

He shrugged and took a heaping bite of pancake.

"You're very humble for a guy with such a big head."

He laughed.

While we finished eating, something occurred to me. "Let me guess," I began. "You were in the process of getting a divorce when all this happened. Then your ex decided she didn't want to be your ex after all."

"How'd you know?"

"Oh, I don't know, by the way she acted like she owned you the other day."

"Well, she doesn't. Taylor and I are over. We have been for a very long time."

"She seems pretty persistent."

He snorted. "She doesn't really want me. I don't make that much more now than I did before my promotion. She just wanted the prestige of my title." He rolled his eyes. "Once she got a look at my bank statement, she would change her mind again."

"Money isn't everything."

He looked up and his face softened. "Yeah, I know."

"Speaking of money," he said and reached into the pocket of his cargo shorts to pull out the card Mr. Goddard gave him. "Are you going to call him and arrange a time to talk?"

"I don't know what to do," I confided, staring off across the restaurant. I noticed the blond woman now had a plate of food in front of her, but she wasn't eating because she had her cell phone pinned to her ear.

"Can I tell you what I think?"

"Please."

"I think you should call him, meet with him later today, and sign the papers. You can take your time deciding if you want to keep the money, but at least this way it will all be in your name."

I puzzled over his words. "Why does that matter?"

"Because once it's all in your name, it's not fair game for anyone else."

I leaned across the table and spoke quietly. "So you think once I take it, whoever's trying to kill me will stop?"

"Seems that way. Right now that money is kind of in limbo. If you die before claiming it, then it's sort of up for grabs. But once it's all in your name, it won't matter if you die because the money will go to whoever you leave it to."

"You're right."

"I know," he said smugly, sitting back in his chair.

"Can I borrow your cell phone?"

After he handed it over, I dialed the number on the card. Mr. Goddard picked up on the third ring. "Hello, this is Katie Parker. We spoke yesterday?"

"Yes, of course, Miss Parker. How are you?"

"I'm fine, thank you. I'm calling to see if we could arrange a time to sign those documents we discussed?"

"Of course. Would this evening work for you? I have a conference call this afternoon."

"Sure. Would six o'clock work for you?"

"That would be fine. Would you like to meet here at the hotel? There is a lounge right off the lobby."

I agreed and then hung up the phone, handing it back to Holt.

"I'm supposed to meet him later at his hotel."

"So we have all day, then?"

"Seems like it."

He grinned and made a call of his own, arranging for us to go somewhere.

"Who was that?" I asked after he requested the bill from the waitress.

He gave me a sly smile. "My mother."

I felt my mouth drop open. He reached across the table and used his finger to snap my jaw closed. "You're going to catch flies."

I narrowed my eyes. "I can't go meet your parents!"

"It's just my mom. Dad's at work."

"No!"

"Why not?" he asked, reaching for his wallet. I snatched the check out of his hand and stuck my tongue out.

"I'll pay."

His eyes narrowed. "Fine. You pay. I'm going to pull the truck around. My mother's expecting us."

Before I could argue further, he was up and pushing through the exit doors. I let out a frustrated sigh and pulled some cash out of my purse. Anxiety made my hands shake as I counted out the correct amount of change. I wasn't ready to meet his mother. I couldn't understand why he was forcing this. We weren't even dating… We were… Well, I didn't know what we were, but it didn't seem like we were at any kid of stage for me to be meeting the parents.

The waitress came back over as the shiny red truck slid to the curb. I handed her the money and told her to keep the change, then stalled by taking another sip of my juice. Over the rim of my glass, my eyes connected with the blonde in the booth.

She was no longer on the phone and she was watching me with an odd sort of glint in her eyes.

Uneasiness obscured my thoughts as I returned the juice to the table and stood. I didn't look back as I left the restaurant, but I swear I felt her eyes follow me until I was out of sight.

20

His parents lived near an inlet, which provided a year-round view of the sea. Their home was a single-story ranch home made up of light-brick exterior, arched windows, and mature landscaping lining the property. The concrete driveway led along the side of the house up to a two-car garage with a walkway leading to the red front door.

Instead of pulling up the driveway, Holt parked out front, at the edge of the street along the green lawn's edge.

"This is a lovely home," I said, looking out my window at the small palm trees that grew in the front. The house was neat and tidy. You could tell it was lived in but it was well maintained by people who cared about it. "I shouldn't be here," I objected for the millionth time.

"You got somewhere better to be?" he asked, arching a dark brow.

He had me there. I had nowhere to be. At least until six o'clock tonight. "I don't understand why you're pushing this."

He turned away from the steering wheel, leaving the engine running so the air continued to cool the interior of the cab. He lifted my hand out of my lap and held it. "If you feel like I'm forcing you do to something you don't want to do, then say the word. I'll take you home."

Home.

Where was that exactly? With him?

My silence must have unnerved him because he sighed. "I know we haven't known each other very long and your life is pretty upside-down right now."

I nodded for him to continue.

"But I want you in my life. Now and after things calm down."

"What are you saying?"

He smiled. "I'm saying I already know what I want. *Who* I want. I don't expect you to know right now. I don't even expect an answer. I just wanted you to know how I feel."

He wanted me. All that longing I felt before swelled up inside me again, making it hard to breathe. I think I wanted him too. I didn't want to have to say good-bye to him.

But I might have to.

If the person out there who wanted me dead had anything to say about it.

How could I promise him a future when I wasn't even sure I would live through today?

"Holt, I—"

"Hold that thought. We've been spotted."

Panic shot through me and I stiffened, glancing out the back window, looking for some kind of dark car like the one that ran me over or the silver BMW of a lawyer who might have lied.

But there were no other cars on the street.

"I think that was a bad choice of words," Holt muttered, placing a kiss to the back of my hand. Then he pointed out my window.

A tall woman with short, dark hair and a smile stood on the sidewalk. When I turned to stare at her, she waved at us and motioned for us to come inside.

"That's your mother?" I asked.

"Yep. See, she's not that scary."

I laughed. "Fine, let's go."

As he came around to help me leap from the cab, I began to worry about my appearance. I was wearing very little makeup, my hair was loose and likely crazy around my shoulders, and I was dressed really casual in the pair of jeans Holt bought me and a loose-fitting tank top.

"You look beautiful," he whispered as if he somehow knew about my inner worry.

She was waiting on the sidewalk when we approached.

"Holt!" she exclaimed as he gave her a big hug. "So happy to see you today!"

"Hey, Mom. Thanks for letting us stop by."

She smacked him in the stomach. "You know you're welcome here anytime."

Then her eyes turned to me. They were that icy light blue, just like Holt's. "You must be Katie."

"Yes, ma'am."

She laughed and flung her arms around me in a warm, welcoming hug, rocking back and forth a little before she pulled away to look at me again. "You are positively gorgeous!" she exclaimed. "And so tiny! Holt here is three times your size!"

"Mom," he groaned and rolled his eyes.

"You have a lovely home," I said, gesturing to the house.

"Thank you. It's hot out here today. Must be at least a hundred degrees in the shade!" She linked her arm through mine and led me to the front door. "Do you like lemonade?"

"Yes, ma'am."

"No more of that ma'am business. You can call me Pam."

I glanced over my shoulder at Holt and he winked. The inside of the house was blissfully cool and very spacious. There was a tiled entryway that led into a great room with a traditional fireplace, wood floors, and wide windows. Pam led us through that room and also through the dining room, which was beside the kitchen.

"Take a seat," she said, finally releasing my arm and pointing to the barstools by the island. I didn't sit down, though. I went straight to the back doors that overlooked a wooden deck and the yard. The yard led straight down to the water where there was a dock for a boat.

"Nice, isn't it?" Holt said, stepping up behind me. I had the urge to lean back against his chest so he would wrap his arms around me. I might have if I wasn't aware of his mother watching us.

"Absolutely," I agreed.

"So, Katie, Holt tells me you're a librarian," his mother said, drawing me away from the view.

"Yes. I like books."

"Me too!"

The conversation turned to books and literature as we drank lemonade and laughed together about Holt's lack of book knowledge. He did, however, offer many opinions on the movies based off the books we talked about.

His mother was open and friendly with an easy smile and a kind eye. I felt at ease and welcome in her home, and it made something in my chest tighten. Not really in a bad way, but a good one.

I excused myself to go to the bathroom, hoping to take a moment and corral the emotion that seemed to bubble up on me at a moment's notice lately. Since I didn't really have to use the facilities, I moved over toward the window, staring out into the side yard.

Being here in this house, it just made everything worse. It made that ache inside me—the longing for something more than I thought I wanted—worse.

One day at a time, I told myself, inhaling a deep breath.

After today, after I signed those documents, I could start rebuilding my life. I could start making some decisions and really thinking about what I wanted.

As I thought, movement out the window caught my eye. It was a car making its way up the street. There was nothing really unusual about a car driving down the street.

Other than the fact it was a dark sedan.

Flashes from almost being run over assaulted me. I glanced back out the window, hoping to get a better look at the car, but it had already moved out of sight.

You're losing it, Katie, I told myself.

Maybe after tonight I would take a vacation and just relax. I would certainly be able to afford it. Once I felt a little more in control, with my emotions in check, I headed back to the kitchen, only to pause at the sound of a new voice.

"Well, where is this girl you haven't shut up about since you pulled her out of that fire?"

"She's in the bathroom, Dad."

"Probably took one look at your mother and is trying to shimmy herself out the window and run away," he said good-naturedly.

"Ed!" Holt's mother gasped, but then she giggled. "I did not scare that girl. In fact, I really like her. She's a timid little thing, but I think time will fix that."

Did that mean she wanted me to stick around a while? I looked at the family photos lining the hall. Many of them were of Holt as a child, grinning toothlessly into the camera. They looked like such a happy family, with wonderful memories.

"Give me ten minutes with her," Holt's dad replied.

"Dad," Holt warned. "She's been through a lot. Go easy on her, would you?"

"I'm just joking, son." He laughed and I stepped out of the hall in time to see him slap Holt on the back.

"Katie," Holt said, stepping away from his parents and taking my hand. "This is my dad, Edward."

"Just call me Ed, honey."

"Hi. It's nice to meet you." I held out my hand and gave his a firm shake.

"That's quite the grip you got there," he said. "For such a shrimp." But he softened his words with a wink.

I laughed.

He was a big man, just like Holt, with wide shoulders and long legs. He had dark hair too, but his was streaked with gray and was a bit longer than Holt's, hanging down to brush against the collar of his shirt.

He was very tan, like he spent a lot of time in the sun, and he had friendly wrinkles around his eyes that made him look like he smiled an awful lot.

"My dad stopped by on his lunch hour. He owns a construction business."

"Oh, what kinds of places do you build?"

"Mostly custom homes, but I'd consider any kind of job."

"Did you build this house?"

"Good heaven's no!" Pam laughed. "He's such a perfectionist it never would have been done. We'd be living in an apartment waiting for it to be finished!"

Pam went to the refrigerator and started piling some cold cuts and cheese on the table. "Katie, honey, hand me that bread over there," she said, pointing to the counter behind me.

I handed it to her and she smiled.

"Holt, I'm making your father a sandwich. Do you want one?"

"I'm starved," he said.

"You just ate!" I exclaimed.

"You ate all my bacon," he accused.

"I did not!" I laughed, reaching in for a slice of bread and throwing it at him.

He snagged it out of the air and took a huge bite. Holt's dad grinned. "I like this one, son. Better not let her go."

"I don't plan on it," he said, giving me a meaningful stare.

I felt my cheeks heat and I made myself busy putting together a sandwich for him.

"Katie, make one for you too," Pam said, handing me the mayo.

"Oh, no. That bacon really filled me up." I grinned slyly.

She laughed as Holt's phone rang in his pocket. "It's the station. I'll take it outside."

He went out on the back deck, leaving me alone with his parents. I wasn't sure I was ready to be alone with them just yet.

I helped his mother put away all the sandwich fixings and then left Holt's sandwich on a plate on the counter.

"Thank you," his mother said, glancing at me.

"For what?"

"I haven't seen him like this in a very long time."

"Like what?" I asked, confused.

"Happy." His dad cut in, eating half the sandwich in one giant bite. Now I knew where Holt got his appetite.

"I have a hard time picturing Holt as anything other than happy." I scoffed.

"Usually that's true. But Taylor, she really did a number on him."

"I met her."

"Then you know what we're talking about," his father said.

I nodded. There was no denying Holt's ex-wife was a piece of work.

His mother placed her hand on my forearm, saying my name softly and causing me to look up. "Holt told us about everything you've been through lately. I just want you to know you are always welcome here, and if there is anything Ed and I can do for you, you just let us know."

Ah, crap.

There came the emotion again.

I swear I was turning into a big fat baby.

"Thank you," I said, my voice ridiculously watery.

His mother pulled me into her arms and hugged me. "Welcome to the family, honey."

"Oh," I said, pulling away. "Holt and I aren't that serious."

Ed just grunted and his mother patted me on the arm like I was confused. Now I saw where Holt got his stubbornness from as well.

Thankfully, the back door slid open and Holt stepped through, still holding his phone and frowning.

"Is something wrong?" I asked.

"I need to go to the station for a while," he said regretfully. Then he looked at me. "I'm sorry."

"Don't be. I told you to go to work this morning."

He seemed torn. Torn between his job and me. I didn't like that. I went to his side and grabbed his arm, ushering him farther into the room. "Just go, do what you need to do."

"I'll make it fast."

I groaned. "I'll be fine."

"She can stay here with us until you're done," Pam said from behind me.

"Oh, you don't have to do that." I argued.

"I know. I want to."

Holt seemed to like this idea and the clouds in his eyes evaporated. "Stay here. Then I won't worry about you being alone."

Three sets of eyes turned to me. Like I was going to argue. Geez, these people were tough!

Holt knew I was beat and he grinned and leaned down and pressed a quick kiss to my lips, right there in front of everyone.

"I'll be back soon."

He reached around me and snatched the sandwich. "Thanks, Mom!" he called and headed through the house toward the front door.

An uneasy feeling came over me when he disappeared from sight. Some kind of gut feeling that made panic claw at my throat and my heart start to race. When the front door closed behind him, images of that dark car driving slowly up the street a few minutes ago flashed behind my eyes.

"Holt!" I cried, rushing out of the room after him. I almost tripped, flying through the living room, but managed not to fall, calling his name again.

I heard his parents call my name and rush after me, but I didn't stop. I had to get to Holt.

I flung open the front door and screamed his name just as he was opening the door to his truck.

"Holt, stop!" I cried, rushing down the steps and onto the sidewalk.

He looked up through the passenger-side window, surprise written on his face. The truck engine turned over as he twisted the key to start it and then he pulled back out to come around the hood and see what I was screeching about.

He never made it that far.

The explosion rocked the ground under my feet and was so loud I thought I might never hear again. I screamed his name and went rushing toward the mess, where pieces of metal and rubber rained from the sky.

I heard his dad and mother yelling, but I didn't look back. I just kept running, right toward the truck that was now nothing but a massive ball of fire.

"Holt!" I shrieked as the heat from the explosion sucker-punched me in the gut. I doubled over, tears streaking my face and sobs rocking my body.

His truck exploded. He was standing next to his truck… Where is he?

Pushing up, I ran forward again, shaking off his dad's hands as he tried to pull me back from the flames. I rushed around the side of the truck, still wailing his name.

That's when I saw him.

He was lying across the street in the neighbor's front yard. He wasn't moving.

I took off running, pounding across the street and falling to my knees beside him. I could barely see because my vision was obscured by smoke and tears. I laid my head on his chest, trying to quiet the sobs ripping from my throat as I concentrated on hearing a heartbeat.

When I heard it, I collapsed across his chest with relieved weeping.

Wiping the tears from my eyes, I sat up, looking down at him, trying to see his injuries. His dad appeared on his other side, taking Holt by the face and asking him to wake up.

He had soot on his face and blood; there was *a lot* of blood. He had a cut above his eye, oozing red all down the one side of his face. I picked up his hand to plead with him to wake up and I noticed his knuckles were all skinned and raw.

"He's breathing," his dad said, placing his ear right next to his mouth. "Paramedics are on their way."

I cried silently, rocking back and forth while holding his hand in my lap. In that moment I knew, I knew there was no denying my feelings for him anymore. I couldn't pretend we weren't serious. I couldn't pretend what I felt was going to go away once my life calmed down.

He was it for me.

There would never be anyone else.

And I was putting him in danger.

You should have let her die. That note had been a warning to him. Not a threat to me. And I made it worse by going back to his house and getting him further involved. There wasn't a single doubt in my mind that the explosion was meant to kill us both and keep me from claiming that money.

He was still bleeding, and I reached up, yanking off my loose tank I wore above a basic white one and then pressing it to the wound, trying to stop the worst of it. "Stay with us," I told him, brushing a hand over his hair.

His dad was no longer staring at Holt but watching me. "He's going to be okay," I whispered. It sounded more like a prayer.

After maybe twenty seconds, I let out a frustrated cry. "Where the hell is the ambulance!"

I heard a vehicle screech to a stop behind us and I turned, ready to yell at them to get over here, but it wasn't the ambulance.

It was the same dark sedan I saw creeping up the street earlier. I noticed the front end was scratched and banged up a little, like it had run into a shopping cart. Whoever was inside was responsible for all this hurt.

Fury lit through me, sweeping over my limbs like a wildfire in a forest, like a match dropped in a puddle of gasoline. It was one thing to mess with me, but it was something else entirely to mess with the man I was head over heels in love with.

Cambria Hebert

"Stay with him," I told Holt's father, motioning for him to apply the pressure to Holt's wound.

Then I got up and marched toward the person who was climbing out of that car.

21

The first thing I saw step out of the car was a pair of white, popular brand-name sneakers. I probably should have been scared. I mean, this was the guy who torched my home, my motel room, attacked me at the library, and tried to run me down with a car.

But I was too angry to feel afraid.

Holt was lying just feet away, unconscious and bleeding because of this psycho.

He unfolded himself from the passenger side of the car, looking at me through a pair of dark sunglasses. On top of the glasses, he wore a baseball cap pulled low on his head. He just stood there for a few long seconds, watching me like he was a lion and I was his prey.

"Hello, William," I said, taking a chance that this was indeed the lawyer that had gone AWOL on his way to deliver papers to me.

"Paul never could keep his mouth shut," the man spat, confirming my suspicions.

I rushed forward, shoving at the open door he stood behind. The door swung shut, knocking him backward into the car. He gave an angry cry as the door squished his legs.

I grabbed the door to swing it open to hit him again, but he kicked it, sending me sprawling backward onto the ground.

"You shouldn't have done that," William spat, reaching down and grabbing me by the hair.

From behind, Holt's father yelled my name.

The lawyer reared back his fist to punch me, but I twisted, letting out a muffled cry as my hair felt like it was being yanked from its follicles. I lunged forward and bit his calf through his pants and he screamed.

"You bitch!" he kicked me, flinging me backward again.

I was so angry I didn't even feel it. I just scrambled back up, ready to lunge at him again.

"We don't have time for this," a voice hissed from inside the car. "Get her and let's go!"

They wanted to take me? Oh no... I couldn't get in that car. If I got in that car, I would be as good as dead.

I rushed backward, not turning my back, but then I stopped, not wanting to lead the crazy ass any closer to Holt.

Thoughts of him flooded my brain, and I looked over my shoulder, wondering if he was still breathing. His father was getting up, stepping over his son's still body and coming to help me.

I didn't want him to get hurt too.

William took advantage of my distraction and hit me in the side of the head with something hard and cold. Huge black dots swam before my eyes, and then I was falling into my captor's arms.

Ed screamed my name and rushed to help me, but then he halted, his eyes widening and looking at me with a helpless expression.

"You come any closer to her and I swear to God, I will shoot him and then you." William waved a gun wildly.

"No!" I cried, my voice sounding more like a pathetic mew. "Hooltttt," I slurred. "Stay awwaaay."

Then I was being towed backward, my bare feet dragging the ground. The last thing I remember is hearing the sound of approaching sirens before everything went quiet.

*   *   *

One good thing about being kidnapped: you didn't have to worry about where the killer who'd been stalking you for weeks was. Why? Because he already hit you in the head, stuffed you into a car, and was currently driving you to some undisclosed location that probably included a hole in the ground and a dentist's chair with straps.

Okay, maybe it was time I lay off on the horror movies.

But at least I knew Holt was safe.

Holt!

Thoughts of him and the explosion had me springing up in the back seat of the dark sedan, only to have my head swim as I sank back down against the seat.

"Oh good, you're awake," William said from the front seat. "We're almost there."

"Sit up and make yourself look presentable!" came a new voice from the driver's seat.

I couldn't see who it was because I was laying with my head behind the seat. I tried to sit up again and my stomach rolled in protest. *I must have a concussion. Crap, how hard did he hit me?*

"How long have I been out?" I asked, thinking again about Holt. I prayed to God the ambulance came and he was safely at the hospital, getting help.

"We're here," the driver said again, pulling into a parking lot. I pushed myself up in the seat and looked out the window. Well, at least it wasn't a hole in the ground.

It was a hotel. The Hampton Inn to be exact.

This was the place I was supposed to meet Mr. Goddard later today.

"What are we doing here?" I asked, reaching up to finger the knot behind my ear. It was very tender and I winced when my fingers probed it. I felt something warm and liquid, and when I pulled my hand away, my fingers were red.

The driver pulled the car into an empty spot near the drive-through awning at the entrance. Then they spun around and pinned me with a nasty glare.

It was the woman from the restaurant this morning.

The one that looked familiar...

I gasped as she pushed back the dark hoodie covering her blond hair. This was the same woman at Target, the one I saw the morning of the hit and run.

"Let me tell you how this is going to go," she said coldly. "The three of us are going to walk into that hotel, get in an elevator, and pay Mr. Goddard a visit. Then you're going to go sign those papers saying you refuse the money."

I opened my mouth to protest, but she cut me off.

"If you so much as look at someone funny inside the lobby, I swear we will shoot you right there and leave you to die. Then we'll start shooting anyone else who's around."

"Why would you do this?" I whispered, horrified by the thought of them shooting innocent people.

"Because that money is ours!" she yelled. "We were the ones who put up with him! We tolerated his arrogance and answered his every beck and call."

We? Who the hell was she? Then I realized… "You're his ex-wife, aren't you?"

"If only I had put up with him a little bit longer, all that money would have been left to me!"

"He left you a house. I have no doubt its worth millions."

She snorted like that was pocket change.

Then I glanced at William. "Tony left you money. Mr. Goddard told me so."

"Over twenty years I worked for him. I covered up his indiscretions. I paid off his drug suppliers when he pissed them off. Hell, I even gave him my piss so he would pass his drug tests!"

"So you enabled him instead of getting him help," I said, suddenly angry again. I may not have known Tony—he might have abandoned my mother when she was pregnant and refused to claim me as his daughter when I was born—but he didn't deserve that. It was all so sad. He was surrounded by people who only used him because they thought it would get them somewhere.

No wonder he left the money to me.

"He was beyond help." William snarled.

I shook my head regretfully. No one was beyond help.

"Let's go," the blonde snapped, pushing open her car door.

William did the same, opening up the back door and reaching in to grab me. Before yanking me from the car, he opened up the suit jacket he was wearing and showed me the gun hidden in his holster. "Remember, I *will* shoot you."

I got out of the car, wobbling a little on my unsteady legs and trying really hard not to double over and vomit right there on the pavement. That would probably get me shot too.

Tony's ex-wife came around the side of the car and linked her arm through one of mine like we were best girlfriends. *Gag.* She'd shed the black hoodie to reveal a skintight black dress to match the sky-high black heels on her feet.

William stuck close to my other side as they led us into the lobby of the hotel. Immediately, I looked around for someone I could alert, for someone I could at least mouth the words "help me" to.

Just my luck the lobby was empty and the only woman behind the front desk was on the phone, staring at a computer screen behind the desk.

They led me to an elevator and then shoved me inside once it dinged open. I hit the back of the elevator wall and bounced off, falling to my knees. Vomit forced its way up the back of my throat, but I swallowed it back down.

"Get up," the woman said, kicking at me. The toe of her shoe bounced off my still tender wrists and I yelped.

"Geez, go easy," William told her.

"Said the man who hit her in the head with a gun."

He had the grace to look sheepish.

Idiot.

The elevator rolled to a stop and William reached down to pull me up by the elbow and anchor me at his side. He half-dragged me into the hall and around the corner.

Unfortunately, the hallway was empty too.

We stopped in front of a door and William knocked.

"Who is it?" Mr. Goddard called from inside the room.

"Answer him," William growled, shoving the gun into my ribs.

"It's Katie Parker, Mr. Goddard," I said, hoping I sounded scared and he would call the police instead of opening the door.

Several seconds later, the door swung open to reveal Mr. Goddard who was dressed in a dark suit and tie. "Katie? I thought we were—" His words cut off when he saw I wasn't alone.

He looked at William. Then the gun. Then he tried to slam the door in our faces, but William slammed his palm on the door and pushed it wide. Then he gave me a rough shove into the room.

Mr. Goddard reached out to steady me. "I'm so sorry," I told him.

"Paul?" came a voice over the speaker of the telephone sitting on the table nearby. "Is something wrong?"

I forgot he was supposed to be doing a conference call this afternoon.

"Help!" I cried. "They have a gun!"

"Paul?" the voice called frantically. "Who is this?"

William charged into the room and yanked the phone cord out of the jack and threw the phone against the wall where it burst into a useless mess.

My only hope was that whomever he was talking to would have enough sense to call the police.

"The papers, Paul! Get the papers!" William said, pointing the gun at the man.

"What papers?" he asked, putting his hands up in the air.

"He wants me to refuse the money," I explained.

Paul's eyes widened as he just stood there and stared at the gun.

The blonde stepped between the gun and Mr. Goddard. "Get the papers, old man," she growled.

He nodded and went across the room to his briefcase, where he shuffled through some papers and pulled out what he was looking for. "This one here is the one you would sign if you did not accept the money," he said, glancing at me and then at William, his mouth flattening into a straight line.

William shoved me toward Mr. Goddard and the papers. "Sign them."

"You do realize even if she signs those papers, you still won't get that money," Mr. Goddard said, his tone haughty and lawyer-like. If I were being questioned by him, I would totally pee my pants.

"You let me worry about getting the money," William said, his eyes bulging in anger.

"How do you plan on getting it?" he asked him curiously. I figured he really didn't care; he was just trying to buy us more time.

I started looking around the room, trying to find something that could potentially be used as a weapon. There wasn't much. This hotel was clutter free and tidy. The lamps were bolted to the walls, and there weren't heavy items like a vase sitting around. Even the TV was a flat screen that was also attached to the wall.

"I'm a lawyer," William bragged. "I'll tie this money up in court until I can find a loophole to make it mine."

"And how do you think you're going to get away with forcing her to sign those papers? For holding us at gunpoint?"

"Let's not forget arson, kidnapping, hit and run, and attempted murder."

"Hit and Run?" William said, looking genuinely confused.

"Shut up! Both of you!" the blonde yelled, grabbing me by the arm and dragging me to the desk. "Sign those!"

"He didn't know you tried to run me over with a car the other day?" I asked her loudly.

"Is that true, Caroline?"

A pretty name for such an ugly person.

"What was I supposed to do, Liam? You were failing miserably. I mean, how hard could it be to kill this mouse of a girl?"

"You didn't manage it either," I snapped.

She backhanded me across the face. It was a solid slap, so solid my ears rang and my skin stung. "Shut. Up."

Dizziness threatened me once again and my stomach churned. I grabbed the edge of the desk to steady myself.

She grabbed up a very nice gold pen off the desk and shoved it at me. "Sign. Now."

I took the pen and spread the papers out on the desk, pretending like I was leaning over them to scrawl my signature.

"I can't believe you didn't trust me!" William yelled, sounding like he might come unhinged at any second.

Caroline turned to her head to answer him and I struck out, bringing the pen up near my shoulder and then swinging it down and plunging it into the soft spot just above her collarbone between her shoulder and her neck.

She howled in pain and stumbled to the side. William cried her name and rushed to her side as he stared at the pen still sticking out of her body. Blood spurted out around it, looking like some sick fountain.

"Go!" I told Mr. Goddard, pointing toward the door. I was stuck behind the desk, but he could go for help.

He ran for the door, but William lunged after him, clubbing him over the head with the butt of the gun. Mr. Goddard sprawled forward and face-planted on the floor.

Please don't let him be dead, I prayed silently.

Then he turned back, a wild and uncontrolled look in his eyes.

Caroline made a sound and yanked the pen out of her body, holding it up and watching the blood drip off the end. "You little bitch," she growled, tossing the pen aside. Blood was pouring down her arm and pooling in the low-cut neckline of her black dress.

She ripped the gun out of William's hands and pointed it steadily at me. "I'm going to kill you."

"Now, Caroline. Wait. She hasn't signed the papers yet."

"I'll forge her name."

William came forward, slipping between me and the gun. "Just wait a second, okay, sugar plum?"

Okay, that's just nasty. He calls that beast of a woman *sugar plum*? The urge to vomit came back full force.

"Hurry up!"

William turned to me.

"I don't have a pen anymore," I said sheepishly. Then I looked around William at Caroline. "So tell me, were you sleeping with William before you married Tony or just when you figured out you might get some money out of it?"

She made a cry of outrage and re-aimed the gun. I saw the decision in her eyes the split second she decided to kill me. In a final attempt to save myself, I leapt to the side as the gun went off, grabbing William around the waist and using him as a shield.

I felt his body jerk as we both landed hard on the floor with him on top of me. He was heavy like a huge block of cement.

"Liam!" Caroline cried, rushing over just as I managed to push him off and roll from beneath him.

He groaned and fell onto his back. His midsection was drenched in blood. "You shot me."

"Oh my God!" she cried and leaned over his body, weeping.

I took the chance to vault myself over the desk, grabbing the papers and rushing toward the door.

"Not so fast," came a voice behind me along with the telltale cocking of the gun.

I froze.

"Turn around," she ordered.

I did, pivoting around and looking at her. She was pale, and the gun wasn't as steady in her hand as it was before. She was still pouring blood and now it coated her hands, but I couldn't tell if it was hers or William's.

"All you had to do was sign one little piece of paper," she said, her voice deadly calm. "We would have let you live. But now... now I'm going to enjoy killing you."

Please. She was such a liar. She and I both knew that they never had any intention of letting me live. Her words were a colossal waste of breath.

"Grab that pen," she gestured to one lying on the nightstand by the bed.

I did as she asked.

"Sign the papers."

I leaned down and used the top of the nightstand to write. When I was finished, I slapped the pen on top of the paper and stood. "There. Money's all yours."

She smiled with satisfaction as I picked up the alarm clock near my hand and threw it at her. It knocked the gun out of her hand, and I leapt at her, shoving her to the floor.

She screamed as I made a run for it, but she caught me around the ankle and yanked, causing me to lurch forward. Mr. Goddard broke my fall. I rolled, trying to kick at her so I could get up. But she outweighed me by at least thirty pounds and she was able to pin me to the floor easily by straddling my waist and using her body weight.

She wrapped her hands around my neck and applied pressure, cutting of my oxygen supply and making my lungs seize with panic.

Calm down, I told myself. *Think!*

I gripped her wrists, trying to pry them off me, but when spots began swimming before my eyes, I decided to try something else. Instead, I reached up and dug my nails into the hole in her shoulder. Her blood was sticky and hot.

She howled in pain, her grip slipping, and I gulped in air greedily. Then I rolled, knocking her off of me and pinning her to the ground. She clawed at me, scraping my arms and pinching my skin. I yanked her hair and drew my fist back to punch her.

But she caught my wrist and squeezed.

I screamed, pain burning up my arm and giving her the advantage of pushing me off her. As I rolled, my head hit the dresser and I gagged from the pain.

My vision got fuzzy around the edges and she leaned over me, her mouth moving as she spoke, but I didn't hear any of it.

This was it.

I was going to pass out and then she would shoot me.

At least I wouldn't be awake when I died.

My eyes began to feel heavy and as they closed, I thought of Holt. Of the future we would never have.

I heard him talking to me, asking me to wake up.

I smiled at the way my brain remembered the exact sound of his voice.

Cold water splashed over my face and my eyes sprang open as I gasped at the icy droplets hitting my skin.

"Katie!" Holt yelled, sliding his hand beneath my head and leaning over me. "Stay with me."

It wasn't my imagination. He was here!

"Holt?" I said, my voice sounding far away.

"Everything's okay now. You're safe."

"You're here," I said.

"Yes, sweetheart, I'm here."

The fog in my brain cleared away and my eyes focused on his face. The cut above his eyebrow was swollen and oozing. He had blood smeared all over his face and his eye was turning a nasty shade of purple.

"Why aren't you at the hospital?" I demanded, trying to sit up but groaning and falling back down.

"Easy," he murmured.

"Hospital," I reminded him.

"I'm not going anywhere without you."

Someone groaned inside the room. It sounded like Caroline, and I gripped Holt's arm. "She has a gun!"

"Not anymore," he said, grim, anger playing across his features.

And then the room was swarmed by police officers and EMTs. Holt picked me up and cradled me against his chest. He sat down on the bed, keeping me in his lap.

Torch

One of the EMTs was leaning over Mr.
Goddard. "This one's alive," he said, looking up at his
partner who was leaning over Caroline.

"She's alive too."

Then he left Caroline's side and went over near
the desk where William was. A few seconds later he
said, "DOA."

A sob ripped from my throat and I clutched
Holt. He gathered me closer against him and
whispered in against my ear that everything was going
to be okay.

I believed him.

"She's got a concussion," Holt called out, and
then there were hands on me that weren't Holt's as
the medics checked my eyes and response.

From on the floor, Mr. Goddard groaned and sat
up, leaning against the wall. "What happened?"

"Caroline shot William. He's dead," I said,
glancing over to where he sat.

"I'm very sorry about all of this," he said sadly.

"So am I."

"It's over now," Holt said, still refusing to let me
go (much to the EMT's frustration).

"What about her?" I said, feeling a twinge of
panic when I looked over to where she lay. "What's
wrong with her?"

"I punched her in the head," Holt said
unapologetically.

"I stabbed her with a pen."

"That's my girl."

I was so relieved we were both still alive. I didn't
bother to remind him not to talk to me like I was a
dog.

Cambria Hebert

A police officer was cuffing her hands behind her back. "She's going to spend a long time in jail."

"They're the ones who have been trying to kill me."

The officer nodded grimly. "There will be plenty of time to get your statement later, after you've been to the hospital."

"You believe me, right?" I worried. What if she got away with this?

He nodded. "Absolutely. There are too many witnesses for her to get out of this."

"If you signed those papers, I will be sure the courts know it was under duress," Mr. Goddard said.

Holt glanced at me. "Did you sign them, Katie?"

I glanced at the documents still on the nightstand. "See for yourself."

He leaned over and grabbed them up, glancing down at the signature line.

His chuckle was a welcome sound.

I glanced down at my "signature."

SCREW YOU.

Then I looked back at Mr. Goddard. "My signature is not on that paper. But I would like to sign the papers to claim the money."

"I have extra copies in my suitcase. I never travel without doubles."

I looked back up at Holt. "You came for me."

He touched my cheek with his fingers. "When I woke up and Dad told me they'd taken you, I about lost my mind."

"I thought you died in that explosion."

"Takes a lot more than that to kill me."

"Thank God." I laid my head against his chest. The EMT sighed and gave up, going to see about Mr. Goddard's injuries instead.

"How did you know where I was?"

"When I came to, Dad told me two people forced you into a car and drove off. I knew it was about the money, and I knew you were meeting the lawyer here. I didn't even wait around for the EMTs to check me out. I took Dad's work truck and sped the entire way. I heard the gunshot as I was getting off the elevator." His voice turned hoarse. "When I burst in here and saw her on top of you, I lost it. I would have killed her if the cops weren't rushing down the hall."

"Thank you for saving me," I whispered, reaching up to cup his jaw.

"You saved me too. If you hadn't come running out of the house, I would have been inside my truck when it blew."

I squeezed my eyes shut at the horrible image.

"How did you know?" he asked.

"I didn't. I just had a really bad feeling all of a sudden. I panicked."

He hugged me closer, hunching around my body. "We came close, Freckles. We almost lost everything."

"But we didn't," I whispered, inhaling his scent that still clung to his skin even after he was the victim of an explosion.

"We need to get you two to the hospital," one of the police officers said, gesturing to the door.

I looked up and noticed that Mr. Goddard and Caroline where already gone and there was a sheet draped over William's body.

Holt stood. When he didn't put me down, I patted his chest. "I can walk."

He shook his head. "You have a concussion."

"So do you," I reminded him.

"Yours is worse."

"Why? Because I'm a girl?" I countered.

"Because I want to hold you."

I couldn't argue with that. So I didn't.

The ambulance was waiting when we stepped outside. Before lifting me up into the back, Holt leaned down and covered my lips with his.

The heat was instantaneous, sweeping up inside me and igniting a fire of passion that only he could make me feel.

"I thought fire fighters were supposed to put out fires, not make them," I said when he lifted his head.

He smiled. "Get used to the heat, sweetheart, because this is one flame I'm never putting out."

I liked the sound of that.

Epilogue

The ringing of the phone cut into my sleep. I untangled myself from Holt's embrace and reached for my brand-new cell phone lying on the nightstand beside the bed. I liked it better when I didn't have a phone to ring and wake me up.

"Hello?" I answered, trying not to sound like I was sleeping in the middle of the afternoon.

"Miss Parker?"

"Yes?" I said, my mind going through the possibilities of who the woman on the other end of the line was.

"My name is Anita Caldwell. I'm with First People's Bank here in Wilmington."

"Oh yes, how are you today, ma'am?"

"I'm doing well. Thank you for asking. I'm calling to let you know that the transfer of your funds has finally been approved. All the money has been deposited into your account and is now available for your use."

"Wonderful, thank you very much."

"It's a pleasure banking with you, Miss Parker."

"Did the other transfers to the other accounts go through as well?"

"Yes, ma'am, everything went through according to the way you set up your accounts."

"Thank you for the call, Mrs. Caldwell."

"If you need anything else, please don't hesitate to come into the bank or call me directly."

"I will."

When the call was disconnected, I tossed the phone toward the end of the bed, hoping it would get lost in the covers and never be seen again.

I felt a gentle hand stroke up the inside of my thigh and I smiled, glancing over at a still "sleeping" Holt.

"That was the bank," I told him as his fingers crept higher, lingering on the edge of my panties. "The money went through."

"So you're filthy rich?" he rumbled, his voice still heavy with sleep.

"Guess so."

He grunted. "I thought it would take longer."

"It's been a couple of weeks."

He didn't say anything, instead slipping his fingers beneath my underwear and teasing the sensitive skin there. My body reacted like it always did when he touched me. Desire pooled deep in my belly, my nipples tightened, and moisture gathered between my legs.

I lay back down, opening up for him, for his touch. "You're trying to distract me," I murmured as one of his fingers slid inside me.

"It's working."

He knew it would. It always did. I knew he didn't want to have this talk—the talk where we decide where our relationship was going. He had kept his word. He'd told me he wasn't trying to pressure me and I didn't have to answer him right away about what I wanted. But every time since then when I tried to bring it up, he silenced me some way or another.

"I know what's going on here," I murmured between a lustful moan.

His reply was to slip yet another finger inside me. "You're scared."

He stilled and lifted his head off the pillow. "Excuse me?"

I thrust myself against his fingers, which were no longer doing what I wanted them to do.

Very carefully, achingly slow, he pulled them out, tugging my panties back into place and pulling his arm from beneath the sheets. Hooking me around the waist, he towed me closer so he was partly lying atop me, tucking his arms around me and playing with the ends of my hair. "You want to talk, Freckles? Let's talk."

I took a breath. "I think you're worried I'm not going to stay here now that I have more than enough money to leave."

I saw the acknowledgement behind his eyes, the insecurity. "I just haven't wanted to push you. You've been through a lot."

"So have you," I whispered, reaching up to lightly trace the slight scar above his eyebrow. Six stitches, that's how many the cut on his head required.

He caught my hand and pressed a kiss to my fingers.

"For as long as I can remember, all I wanted was a solitary life, a life where I only had to worry about me and I wouldn't have to worry about someone leaving me or hurting me."

He opened his mouth to say something, but I shook my head and he fell silent.

"But then my house caught on fire and everything changed." I smiled. "It wasn't really in your job description to come visit me every day at the hospital, was it?"

He shook his head. "I couldn't stay away. I hated seeing you lying there like that."

"I love you, Holt."

He sucked in a breath, staring down at me with those incredible blue eyes. "Katie—"

"I have for a while. I was just too afraid to tell you. But I'm not scared anymore. I love you and I want a life with you. I hope you still want that too."

His mouth was on me before I even finished saying the words. He crushed me against him, holding me so closely I wasn't sure where my heartbeat ended and his began. I gripped his shoulders, holding on as sensation after sensation rippled through my body as his mouth moved over mine again and again.

Then he was between my legs, burying himself inside me with one great thrust and making me cry out with need.

"Look at me, Katie," he demanded, holding himself above me with his elbows.

I forced my eyes open and looked up. "I love you."

And then he began to move—slow, sinful strokes, in and out, in and out—until I was panting with anticipation.

Neither one of us lasted much longer, both tumbling into ecstasy at the same moment. I felt him pumping into me, and the intimacy of that single act had my heart squeezing with joy. He collapsed on top of me but caught himself and stiffened, trying to roll away so he wouldn't crush me.

I made a sound of protest and pulled him back, wrapping my legs around him to keep him close. I wasn't quite ready to break our contact just yet.

"Shit," he swore softly into the pillow beside my head. "I forgot to use a condom." He gazed down at me. "I'm clean, I swear."

I smiled. "Guess it's time to get on the pill."

"Just the thought of my child growing inside you thrills the shit out of me."

"Me too."

"Yeah?" he said hopefully.

I nodded. "But I'd like to have you all to myself for just a little bit longer before we start thinking about that."

"Deal," he said and moved in to kiss me, but before he could, he drew back. "I love you."

"I love you, too."

"I don't want you to move out."

"Me either. I talked to your dad. He's going to rebuild my house and then I'm going to sell it. This is my home now."

The look on his face made my heart turn over.

"But," I warned, "I am going to be buying some more furniture for this house."

"I don't care. You can paint the whole place pink if it makes you happy."

"You make me happy."

This time he did kiss me.

"Holt? There's something else I want to talk to you about," I said when he lifted his head.

"What?"

"I want to use some of the money Tony left me to open up some sort of home or program for foster kids. I don't ever want them to feel the way I did when I was moving through the system."

In the end, I decided to keep the money. I broke it up into several accounts so it wasn't all sitting in one huge sum. I decided instead of just donating it all (but I did donate some), I would use it to make some of my own dreams come true. And Holt didn't know it, but he was getting a brand-new truck.

"That's a great idea. You're going to change a lot of kids' lives."

"The way you changed mine."

He shook his head. "I didn't change your life. You did."

"I couldn't have done it without you."

"I almost forgot," he said, getting up out of bed and going to his dresser. "I have something for you."

"You do?" I pushed up to lean against the headboard.

He nodded and handed me a small velvet sack. I took it and gave him a curious look, then dumped the contents out onto my palm.

"Oh my…" I gasped, looking up at him. "How did you…?" And then I promptly burst into tears.

He gathered me into his arms and held me until the heaviest of my sobs subsided, and then I leaned away to hold my palm up between us. Brilliant sparkling silver shined up at me.

It was my mother's necklace.

One of the very last things I had left of her. It was a locket, a silver heart with my birthstone in the center. My shaking hands fumbled with the heart until I got it open, fresh tears forming when I saw the picture of her and me was still inside.

"I thought I lost this in the fire," I whispered, running a gentle finger over our smiling faces.

"I went to the house and dug around through the rubble, and it was there. Still in one piece. The clasp was broken and it was covered in soot, so I had it cleaned up at the jewelers."

"You have no idea how much this means to me," I said, gripping the necklace in my hand. It was like that piece of her I thought I lost, the piece I'd been grieving since the night of the fire, was back. Now I had this and her letter to Tony (I still wasn't ready to think of him as my father) to remember her by.

I wrapped my arms around his neck, hugging him tightly. "Thank you, Holt. Thank you so much."

"Thank you," he said softly, pulling back and wiping away a stray tear on my cheek.

"For what?"

"For withstanding the heat. For fighting for your life. Because without you, everything in my life would be cold."

I smiled. "You don't ever have to worry about that. There will always be a fire burning between us."

And there was.

The End

Cambria Hebert

Keep an eye out for TEASE, the next *Take It Off* novel, in September 2013!

You can look, but you can't touch…

Harlow is a broke college student. When her tuition assistance is taken away, she is faced with a choice: admit to her mother she couldn't hack it on her own or make a lot of money fast.

So she gets a good-paying job.

As a stripper.

She thought it would be easy, but it turns out being sexy is a lot harder than she thought. When a few mishaps work in her favor, she manages to hang on to her job and catch the eye of the Mad Hatter's best-looking bartender, Cam.

She's also caught the eye of someone who wants to do more than look, someone who's decided she's nothing but a tease.

As the clothes come off, Harlow finds herself caught between lust and murder. The only thing she knows for sure is that her new risqué job is a lot more than she bargained for.

Cambria Hebert

ACKNOWLEDGEMENTS

I would like to thank the Academy for this shiny award that weighs more than my head... Oh wait... this isn't some speech that bores everyone and their mother to death. This is the part where I ramble on about everything I did while writing this book and then I pull out a long list of names to thank people.

Oh, you don't want to read that either?

Too bad.

Okay, I will keep the list to a minimum. In actuality, this book took a lot less time to write than I thought it would. TORCH was my very first attempt at a new adult contemporary novel. I was excited to try a new genre (my other books are all paranormal), but I was also a little reluctant. Reluctant = me messaging my writer buddies Cameo Renae and Amber Garza to belly ache about how hard it is to write a new adult contemporary novel. Everyone kept telling me how easy they were to write, but I didn't seem to grasp it at first. I guess I was so used to hellhounds and men that worked for the Grim Reaper that writing normal people was beyond my grasp.

Side note: another reason writing "normal" people is difficult for me is because I highly doubt I have ever been considered normal. Ha-ha.

But I just decided to dive in and give it a go. I figured if it didn't turn out well, I could hide the pages under the bed and pretend it never happened. OR I could call up the Grim Reaper (he and I are buds) and have him come take care of the mess I made.

Fortunately for me (and Holt and Katie), I didn't have to do any of that. Turns out writing TORCH was really fun. I love the way these characters mesh. Holt is like a giant anchor and Katie is like a boat lost at sea. I love the simplicity of the story but how entertaining it is (at least I hope I'm not the only one who thinks this).

I would first like to give special acknowledgement to Jessica Sorensen, who took time out of her incredibly busy schedule to read this book and graciously allowed me to quote her on the cover. Thank you so much, Jessica, for doing that. I know that you have a very demanding release schedule and it's so awesome that you took time out of your life to give me a hand.

I would like to acknowledge Amber Garza and Cameo Renae (you should read them—they rock) for being there to cheer me on. You two ladies are so awesome. I appreciate you both so much. Special thanks to Amber, who read TORCH for me to give me some early feedback and help calm some of my nerves about the book.

To Regina Wamba of Mae I Design, thank you so much for sharing your incredible talent with me and everyone in the book world. Your design of TORCH is so incredible. I sometimes just stare at it and sigh. It is everything I wanted in a new adult cover and I can't thank you enough for giving TORCH the heat it deserved.

Also, to Cassie McCown of Gathering Leaves Editing, thank you so much for fixing all my bad habits, for always being on time, and for doing your job so well. An editor like you is extremely hard to find, and I feel really lucky that we have the chance to work together. Someday I will break my habit of using the word "that" in every sentence I write. Until then, keep your shovel handy.

I would also like to give a shout out to the girls of Girls *Heart* Books for organizing a three-day release day blitz and an upcoming *Take It Off* tour. You ladies have been so wonderful to work with. Thank you for your support!

I couldn't have written this book without the support of my Nespresso machine. Thank you for making me too many wonderful lattes every single day. I seriously have no idea how I survived without you.

And as always, to my husband Shawn, without you I wouldn't be able to do what I do. Thank you for always being there for me and our kids. We love you.

And that concludes this book's acknowledgements! See you next book!

Torch

Cambria Hebert is the author of the young adult paranormal *Heven and Hell* series, the new adult *Death Escorts* series, and the new adult *Take it Off* series. She loves a caramel latte, hates math, and is afraid of chickens (yes, chickens). She went to college for a bachelor's degree, couldn't pick a major, and ended up with a degree in cosmetology. So rest assured her characters will always have good hair. She currently lives in North Carolina with her husband and children (both human and furry), where she is plotting her next book. You can find out more about Cambria and her work by visiting
http://www.cambriahebert.com

"Like" her on Facebook:
https://www.facebook.com/pages/Cambria-Hebert/128278117253138
Follow her on Twitter:
https://twitter.com/cambriahebert
Pinterest:
https://pinterest.com/cambriahebert/pins/
GoodReads:
http://www.goodreads.com/author/show/5298677.Cambria_Hebert

Cambria Hebert

ALSO CHECK OUT THESE EXTRAORDINARY AUTHORS & BOOKS:

Alivia Anders ~ Illumine
Cambria Hebert ~ Death Escorts Series (Recalled & Charmed)
Angela Orlowski Peart ~ Forged by Greed
Julia Crane ~ Freak of Nature
J.A. Huss ~ Tragic
Cameo Renae ~ Hidden Wings
A.J. Bennett ~ Now or Never
Tabatha Vargo ~ Playing Patience
Tiffany King ~ Meant to Be
Beth Balmanno ~ Set in Stone
Lizzy Ford ~ Zoey Rogue
Ella James ~ Selling Scarlett
Tara West ~ Visions of the Witch
Heidi McLaughlin ~ Forever Your Girl
Melissa Andrea ~ The Edge of Darkness
Komal Kant ~ Falling for Hadie
Melissa Pearl ~ Golden Blood
Alexia Purdy ~ Breathe Me
L.P. Dover ~ Love's Second Chance
Sarah M. Ross ~ Inhale, Exhale
Brina Courtney ~ Reveal
Amber Garza ~ Star Struck
Anna Cruise ~ Maverick